His Secret Little
Wife

His Secret Little
Wife

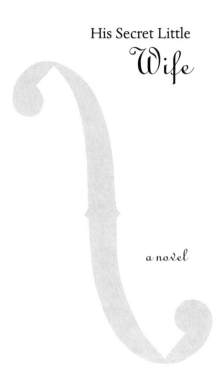

a novel

Fredrica Wagman

STEERFORTH PRESS • *Hanover, New Hampshire*

For Howard, whom I've loved so much and for so long . . . and for my brother Chuck, with love.

Copyright © 2006 by Fredrica Wagman

ALL RIGHTS RESERVED

For information about permission to reproduce
selections from this book, write to:
Steerforth Press L.C., 25 Lebanon Street,
Hanover, New Hampshire 03755

Library of Congress Cataloging-in-Publication Data

Wagman, Fredrica.
 His secret little wife : a novel / Fredrica Wagman. — 1st ed.
   p. cm.
 ISBN-13: 978-1-58642-116-8 (alk. paper)
 ISBN-10: 1-58642-116-6 (alk. paper)
 I. Title.

PS3573.A36H57 2006
813'.54—dc22

2006015280

This novel is a work of fiction. Names, characters, places, and incidents either are the products of the author's imagination or are used fictitiously. Any resemblance to actual persons, living or dead, events, or locales is entirely coincidental.

FIRST EDITION

"I'm what happened."
ENID BAGNOLD

"I see myself as a servant of all the great composers — this is the conductor's role, to serve the music — not himself."

OTTO VON OCHSENSTEIN

part one

one

They lived next door . . . on the other side of the high green privet hedge that separated their world from ours . . . the first time I saw him he was standing on their terrace looking into our garden through binoculars — enormously tall and thin with very white skin and no hair, not even then, not one hair on his long bald head, making him completely colorless as though he were a statue — Otto von Ochsenstein! — the world-famous composer, pianist and the famed conductor of the Philadelphia Philharmonic, then, the greatest symphony orchestra in the world.

I was not quite eleven when they moved into the huge white house on the other side of the hedges, that great white stucco mansion set at the top of long sweeping lawns, old copper beech trees, every kind of fruit tree . . . even a small peach orchard in the back with a fish pond in there that in the autumn was the color of opals in the sun — and raised on a small hill on the side of their house directly facing ours, a trellised arbor that in the summer was heavy with purple grapes latticed around a sprawling redbrick terrace, which was where I would often see him looking into our garden through those black binoculars.

In those days, blinded by youthful awe and by the agonizing mistake that there are such people among us who are better — greater . . . more deserving . . .

everything on their side of those high green hedges that separated their lawn from ours seemed as though it were from a completely different planet — so different in fact, that to push my way through and cross over onto their property was to cross into another world . . . a wild, resplendent world extreme in a variety of such astonishing ways as to be completely terrifying . . . extreme in the genius of the world-famous conductor Otto von Ochsenstein and the aristocracy of intellect that that world reflected . . . extreme in wealth and fame and celebrity and the enormous power that came with it . . . extreme not only in the ravishing beauty of the Maestro's wife, Charlotte Hec . . . but in the beauty of their home and their art and their grounds and their gardens, making them in their white stucco palace on the other side of the hedges, with all their dogs and cars and servants . . . their chauffeur Crump, the cook, the butler and all the maids as close to royalty as one could get as their daughter Juliet and I, compatriots . . . bound by the love we had for each other, that first great love affair would lie together on the grass through the long green summers of childhood . . . making fun of everything, telling secrets and laughing.

two

Juliet's mother was one of the great beauties of her time — maybe one of the most beautiful women in the world as well as one of the world's most famous ballerinas . . . Charlotte Hec, granddaughter of the violinist Vladimir Hec, daughter of the world-renowned brain surgeon Stanislav Hec . . . but most astonishing was how beautiful she was . . . that rare kiss of the gods . . . envied above all else as she sat glowing like a jewel set high in all her luminous radiance, exuding an adhesive magic just because you looked at her, an almost humiliating magic as she bent and twisted you as though she were a scorching flame that could shape and reshape anything simply by smiling, until even the smallest child couldn't stop staring at her, transfixed . . . that kind of exquisiteness . . . that kind of magic . . . and yet with something more, something else . . . some other quality smeared across her face that was beyond beauty . . . something vulnerable that made her almost too exquisite to bear . . . to look at Charlotte Hec was somehow like stealing something . . . doing something you weren't supposed to do . . . the ephemeral marvel of her gorgeousness languishing next to Time . . . that little laughing urchin behind every tree . . . because unlike a gorgeous painting or a sublime piece of sculpture that would never change . . . she would change like flowers change . . . and like seasons change . . . which was part of the sad magnificence of those exquisite vaselike cheeks — her flat long planes of face, her vacant, heavy-lidded amber eyes and long, pitch-black hair piled on top of her head with diamond butterflies . . . what it must be like to see that face every time you look in a mirror . . . pass a window . . . what it must be like to have hair like that — hands like that . . . even her hands were works of art . . . what it must be like to conquer just by walking in a room — every room — while the Maestro sat glowering at the other end of the table — a tight, angry look on the pale white face of this enormously towering presence — thin, bald as an egg — not one hair on his long shiny head . . . even then . . . even when we were children . . . making him look like a long carved piece of alabaster . . . I had just turned eleven when I was ushered for the first time into that mirrored dining room with the three huge drooping crystal chandeliers where they both were presiding, one at each end of a long glass table — she, in a white satin dressing gown with a gigantic diamond ring and three diamond butterflies in her pitch-black hair . . . while the great conductor was sitting sidewise at the other end of the table, his legs crossed, wearing a deep blue satin robe with a bright green satin scarf around his neck — his arms folded staunchly across his chest — glaring at me . . . a shy frightened child . . . as the terror of that whole unimaginable world . . . the terror of Charlotte Hec's raging beauty — the terror of the renowned Otto von Ochsenstein! — his genius, his fame, his incredible wealth . . . and intense glaring face

. . . all of it paralyzing me as I stood trembling in front of him as he kept glaring at me as he kissed my hand.

Now, only the reporter of that world, long gone . . . the exquisite Charlotte Hec, a portrait in a basement of a convent . . . the legendary Maestro, a haunting memory . . . the white stucco mansion on the other side of the high green privet hedge . . . the dogs . . . the servants . . . the art . . . the cars . . . all of it gone to time and taken . . . once long ago I was part of it . . . too much a part of it . . . so much a part of it that maybe I should have run . . . only I didn't run . . . it wasn't in my nature to run any more than it was in Juliet's because maybe children don't know how to run . . . or can't.

three

"May I have your attention *please!*" the great conductor demanded as he began tapping his glass with his long silver luncheon knife to quiet everyone, this time in a yellow satin robe with a bright red satin scarf around his neck, the pale skin on his completely hairless head gleaming as though it had been shined with Turtle Wax as he sat at the head of that long glass table, his three sons by his former wife at the far end while he sat at his end surrounded by only women . . . his daughter Juliet and I, his secretary Gazelle Dimitri-Corson — both sisters of Aunt Charlotte, both beautiful in the same way as she and yet by comparison, and only by comparison, next to Aunt Charlotte, they were so strangely plain that it made the wonder of her beauty even more confounding . . . the Maestro's two sisters, both of them maiden ladies who looked like two great birds of prey, a vulture and a raven with the same long faces as the Maestro only they had great shocks of big dyed hair, wigs probably, one black and the other flaming red next to his ancient withered mother, the old Polish countess Anka Koslowski von Ochsenstein wrapped in countless shawls with fragile blue transparent tissue-paper hands that had an enormous ring on every crooked finger, a black mustache, whiskers and little beady hawk eyes that flashed around looking for a hint — any little telltale sign of something that might be suspicious ; "there's something I want you all to understand," the Maestro began in his most public voice as he continued tapping his glass as he got slowly up from his seat to achieve his full towering height as he began staring sightlessly ahead of himself as though he were addressing, not his family gathered for their usual Sunday luncheon, but rather, the thirty five hundred faces that packed the city's magnificent Academy of Music where every seat for every concert since von Ochsenstein arrived from Chicago was always completely sold out . . . "Music," he said as he cleared his throat . . . "is the great distillation of the livingness of the composer — and not, as some might think, a nourishment for the soul — oh no," he said as he kept looking straight at me — "it is a revelation of the livingness of the genius who created it, and although it cannot bring this livingness to others," he said as he kept staring at me as he was speaking, "it can show that such a livingness exists . . . Bon Appetit!" the Maestro said . . . as the great von Ochsenstein took a small bow as everybody began clapping politely, took his seat and began to eat . . . the great composer and world-famous conductor of the Philadelphia Philharmonic — Otto von Ochsenstein! — the astonishing pianist, magnificent orator and master showman . . . looking around for a moment for something that was not forthcoming — that was never forthcoming from his family — his sisters, his sisters-in-law and his mother listening bored, his three sons at the other end of the table talking and laughing the whole time he was speaking, while Aunt Charlotte . . . distracted by her own deep waters, always distracted, always only half there anyhow, was smiling magnificently as she gazed off into space — entirely disconnected.

four

I must have still been eleven that day, the one that stands out so clearly . . . the memory like a little island . . . unattached . . . still floating through time without a shadow . . . the Maestro, accompanied by a short silent little man, both of them in gray business suits walking toward me . . . it had been raining so I was soaked through — my dress and my hair plastered to me as I was waiting for Juliet at the far end of their living room next to the two concert grand pianos which stood back to back, as though they were curved from the same massive piece of ebony — their huge black wings that day raised for flight . . . as Otto von Ochsenstein and the short silent little man kept walking toward me . . . *"this one! — this is the one! — Look at This!"* the Maestro whispered to the silent little man as they both stood in front of me — the Maestro's thick lidded heavy ice blue eyes like the shining eyes of an iguana, or a crocodile . . . his huge towering height . . . his pale colorless skin and completely hairless head . . . mingling with the terrifying knowledge of who he was . . . *Otto von Ochsenstein! . . . the world-famous composer! . . . pianist! . . . Otto von Ochsenstein! . . . the world-renowned conductor of the Philadelphia Philharmonic!* as he came closer, clasped me by the shoulders and looked into my eyes as he whispered . . . *"never apologize for this beauty, never cringe — never be ashamed . . . because whether you know it or not,"* he said as he kept holding me — *"this is what everything in the universe hungers for,"* he was whispering, his face so close to mine that I could feel his breath.

And as I listened . . . and understood . . . in the way that children who are precocious in some seamy way always understand . . . and as I watched him staring at me . . . and felt the strength of his grip on my shoulders . . . I began to understand what power is.

five

We lived in an old fieldstone house on the other side of that high privet hedge, a simple very old house with nothing exceptional about it except its age, a long front porch and remarkably beautiful gardens that were as bountiful, innocent and silent as the woman who tended them . . . my grandmother, who scratched and dug out there when she wasn't teaching, either in our house or at the prestigious Curtis Institute . . . all day sometimes, bent over with her hoe, patting, planting and pulling each little thing, as brown and as lined and as expressionless as the earth she always had her bare hands in . . . the earth, that gave her that peculiar dry mushroom smell that filled every room she silently entered . . . this slight, frail mindful woman, who in her childhood in Prague was destined for the concert stage — a prodigy, who at the age of seven began studying with the great cellist Maestro Oskar Stigl, but because of the war the family left . . . she taking the cello that Maestro Stigl had given her . . . and although she never played on the concert stage as he had expected — she became a famous teacher . . . and I, her prized student from the time I was old enough to hold a bow was where she put her greatest dreams, her highest hopes — dreams and hopes I never shared . . . and as much as I loved her, when she was old she became stone deaf . . . and this made me ashamed.

∞

My father, Leonard Gold, her son-in-law . . . was a surgeon, a professor of medicine and a medical inventor who devised the famous Gold Clamp — the first to make inroads into the understanding of blood coagulation, the dangers of heavy bandaging and its relation to high fevers, he was a leading expert on sulfa drugs, bacterial infections and peritonitis, as well as an authority on fevers, sub-normal, persistent and uncontrollable but none of this made even the slightest difference to my mother — it didn't matter . . . nothing did . . . not my grandmother's enormous gifts as a musician and as a teacher, or any of my father's contributions, achievements, long list of accolades or all the honors that were heaped on him all his life — none of this counted because my mother wanted *action! endless thrills! — Life!* . . . this small thin, highly charged woman, Kosi Gold, my remarkable grandmother's only child — a wild hybrid with her endless stream of cigarettes, dyed straight black hair and her fierce rage to live — this thirst — this hunger that made her restless, dissatisfied and overly pushy because her burning passion *"to live life to the hilt!"* never found a way — what drove my mother was *excitement!* like the brilliant world of glamour and fame flourishing on the other side of the hedges that made her mad with ambition from the instant the von Ochsensteins moved in . . . and this drive . . . this ravenous hunger for *"Everything!"* as she put it . . . made the mysterious sense of shame I carried, even more unbearable.

six

Our bedroom, my grandmother's and mine, with its dingy organdy curtains, gray and stiff from neglect, our twin beds — our little night table and my desk and desk chair, faced directly into the Maestro's music room on their second floor, which was a huge room with a black concert grand piano and a piano bench, where the Maestro would sit for hours every day practicing or composing in front of a long wall of glass windows that looked out over their latticed terrace — over the hedges . . . over their long sprawling lawns, their swimming pool with the high diving board and into our bedroom, my grandmother's and mine . . . and every night . . . after the concert at the Academy . . . when everyone in both houses was sleeping — I'd turn my head slowly toward the window . . . terrified and excited . . . because there . . . on the other side of the night . . . every night . . . night after night . . . I would see *Otto von Ochsenstein! . . . the great composer! — pianist! and famed conductor of the Philadelphia Philharmonic!* in a satin dressing gown with a satin scarf around his neck, peering into our bedroom through heavy black binoculars.

seven

At exactly seven thirty every morning Anna Marie Vaccaro and I would scramble into the back of the von Ochsenstein's long black Chrysler limousine where Juliet would be waiting with their chauffeur Crump, a huge black man with a gigantic stomach and a loud blustering hee-haw laugh that he laughed all the time, at anything, it didn't matter . . . then Crump would start up the motor, his day beginning by taking Juliet, me and Anna Marie Vaccaro, a quiet, pimply, morose classmate, all of us in white shirts, gray skirts, maroon neckties, high white socks and blue-and-white saddle shoes to a Catholic convent school near the Narberth train station, the Academy of Saint Theresa of Avila, an enormous formidable gray stone compound, a village almost, behind big iron gates surrounded on all sides by gray trees, gray fields, and gray stone walls that separated the church, the vestry, Greenley Academy for Boys and the convent where the nuns lived from our school . . . Saint Theresa's, where we had our first exposure to a kind of cruelty that was so vast — so palpable — that it seemed like cruelty itself was a breathing living entity . . . something howling though the halls, terrifying in its magnitude . . . and yet with a horrible fascination too that made it hard to take our eyes away when a nun would suddenly turn on one of the girls in a pitch of wild rage . . . often Anna Marie Vaccaro because she was slow, or me because I was a Jew, the only Jew in our class and most of the time the only Jew in the school, and as such the nuns blamed me . . . Hannah Elizabeth Gold, the little dark-haired kike in fourth grade . . . who singularly — alone, and all by herself — killed Jesus Christ . . . something always on all their faces that was rigid, with edges made of steel — something fixed and unyielding when they'd look at me silently confronting my every move, my every gesture, my every effort with so much glowering hatred — I was up against something so resolute, so unrelenting, so invincible that every time I walked through those big iron gates . . . day after day . . . the days rolling into months . . . into years, their on-going silent condemnation either eroded or toughened me or maybe both, but slowly, over time it began to make me strangely shameless . . . as painfully ashamed as I was by my grandmother's deafness and of how pushy my mother was, some brazen impenetrableness began to flourish under the nuns' menacing glares, as if to say that no matter what they did I wouldn't feel it . . . they couldn't hurt me . . . not by the way they'd look at me or by the way they called on me in class or by the way they'd pull me out of the lunch line by my ear and make me sit on my hands instead of eating that day because a shoelace wasn't tied . . . but tough as I acted . . . as tough as I seemed . . . I never got past the terror I had of them . . . a terror when they looked at me . . . a terror of their voices . . . a terror of being accused of something I not only didn't do but didn't comprehend and yet assuming the guilt for it automatically . . . like the part in my hair not being straight . . . for killing Christ . . . for not clipping my nails short enough . . . for killing Christ or not turning in a homework assignment on time until I built up a wall around myself that was so thick, so impenetrable — so opaque, that finally nothing they could do could touch me or reach me, not anymore . . . they didn't exist — ghosts I moved among watching them in all their hideous unreasonableness — and in some funny way . . . grieving.

For Juliet, my closest friend, maybe the closest friend I'd ever have, things were different; first of all she was only half Jewish, and that was on her mother's side . . . and more, she was the child of fame, which made a huge impression on everyone, including all the nuns . . . and even more, Juliet was a star in her own right because she was easily the most brilliant student Saint Theresa's had ever had, leaving for boarding school at thirteen and then at sixteen leaving boarding school for Radcliff, but leaving by then in pieces, shattered . . . destroyed in increments, almost imperceptibly . . . born with it all, she was a funny, hardy little girl filled with poetry, joy, enormous faith and an instant ability to forgive . . . then, little by little, destroyed first by Aunt Charlotte, the magnificent ephemeral beauty who was as remote and as unreachable as the enormous portrait of her above the fireplace in the living room . . . then by her father, the golden god of music, Otto von Ochsenstein who was completely indifferent to her, completely unconcerned . . . he simply didn't care, his dose of vanity, anger, fear and a complete absence of compassion was too huge in him to allow him to care very long for anyone . . . then came a place like Saint Theresa's where for the smallest thing even Juliet, an almost perfect student was dishonored, humiliated, her spirit attacked in the name of "what was best for her" because Saint Theresa's was one of those hideous institutions of organized cruelty where sadism was free to flourish under the guise of piety and duty, otherwise known as religion, a monstrous cover-up for all forms of vicious inhumanity that according to those who dispensed it is sanctioned not only by God but by all the Saints . . . sudden beatings, slaps across the face or on the back of the head by those whom we were expected to respect and honor, our teachers . . . or being locked in black closets which was represented as proper treatment for "bad little girls" who dared to giggle, speak out of turn or whisper in class, and always with the injunction "this is for your own good" as the nuns, some so vicious that they exercised their righteous duties with too much zeal — too much vigor, too much lust, not unlike the police who are out there to protect us from their kind, not ours, or our highly trained, greatly esteemed legal prosecutors who are out for blood, not justice — killers all of them . . . with finally capital punishment gleaming like a blazing ruby at the end of all their narrow little tunnels . . . vengeance met with vengeance, blood with blood . . . but we didn't know this then . . . then we trusted as we walked through those big iron gates every morning, Juliet, Anna Marie Vaccaro and I . . . down the long gray path and into that thick gray stone building where we accepted what we had to accept simply and without question because children don't really know their teachers are sadistic psychopaths any more than they know that their parents are crazy . . . they have an inkling, but they don't really know . . . and so, in looking back we say that we were happy and that childhood was a happy time because as children we were in love with life and filled with so much hope we assumed our childhoods had to be happy because being in love with life and being full of hope is a happy state . . . but it was a delusion . . . all of it in our desperate struggle to stay afloat as Anna Marie Vaccaro and I in our white shirts, short gray skirts, maroon neckties, high white socks and blue-and-white saddle shoes scrambled into the back of the von Ochsensteins' long black Chrysler limousine every morning to join Juliet, who was doing all of her homework in the twenty-two minutes it took to get to school, then getting straight A's, one hundreds and gold stars while the rest of us struggled; the work load was enormous which was one of the reasons why St. Theresa's was supposedly one of the great schools for girls in the city, and even though we all got by one way or another (in my case almost out of spite), none of us was anything like Juliet von Ochsenstein, not even in the same breath as she as she sat in the back of her father's long black Chrysler limousine, her shoes and socks on the seat beside her while her bare feet were feeling the softness of the white fur rug on the limousine floor as she scribbled away . . . Juliet wasn't beautiful like her mother, nor was she the Maestro's only child — she had three older half-brothers — and nor was she her father's favorite — Daniel von Ochsenstein was, her father's handsome youngest son . . . and since *"beauty, whether you know it or not,"* according to von Ochsenstein, *"is what everything in the universe hungers for,"* — for the Maestro and for Charlotte Hec, Juliet didn't exist . . . she, like her aunts and her ancient grandmother looked exactly like the Maestro . . . the same extremely pale white skin, unusually pale . . . the same long oval head, the same hawkish nose and thick lidded, light blue eyes, making her an almost perfect replica of the world-famous composer, pianist and renowned conductor . . . *Otto von Ochsenstein!* — Every night his enormous towering stature in black tails with a stiff white shirt and tie, a bright square of light gleaming on the top of his head as he walks out on stage to the thunderous applause of a completely packed house . . . then taking his bow . . . again . . . and then again . . . and then stepping up onto the podium . . . his back to the audience as he whispers what he whispers before every concert — every encore like a prayer . . . *"The Music!"* he begs his musicians — *"Not for me! — Do it for The Music!"* he whispers . . . as he leaps to his toes as his arms come up in a great sweeping circle, his open hands curling in toward his face like claws (*as a memory . . . swift and fleeting . . . of me in a little yellow sundress . . . my father . . . holding me by both wrists so tight I couldn't move*) . . . as the Maestro brings down his arms — and the music begins!

eight

(a memory . . . swift and fleeting . . . of me in a little yellow sundress . . . my father . . . holding me by both wrists so tight I couldn't move . . .) as I began waiting . . . every night . . . for Maestro von Ochsenstein to appear in front of his window . . . and every night . . . like clockwork . . . after every concert . . . he appeared in a satin robe with a satin scarf around his neck and began peering through heavy black binoculars into our bedroom, my grandmother's and mine . . . never knowing, never dreaming for a single second . . . that the prey had begun watching the predator . . . watching him, every afternoon as he was standing on top of the low brick wall that went all the way around their terrace peering into our garden through heavy black binoculars when I was out there with my grandmother . . . watching him . . . in a gray tweed jacket with a red satin scarf tucked in his shirt in the early evening . . . now every evening . . . standing at the top of their high diving board . . . peering into our kitchen through those heavy black binoculars when I was in there with my grandmother and Ida Jenks, and this went on day and night . . . night and day . . . week in — week out . . . until it began to feel like something was always happening . . . a whole new exciting "other" life was going on inside the usual one . . . with some kind of secret promise . . . a kind of secret vow like an unspoken covenant at the very core . . . springing up between Maestro von Ochsenstein and me! — a little dark-haired girl who just by chance lived in the shadow of the big white sprawling mansion on the other side of the hedges . . . who was so awed by him, so stunned and dazzled that in his presence I would tremble and not be able to speak . . . me! — this dark-haired girl . . . still a child . . . yet never a child . . . and he knew it . . . where a window on my soul should have still been shut in innocence . . . it was always — had always been wildly open . . . (as a memory . . . swift and fleeting . . . of me in a little yellow sundress . . . my father . . . holding me by both wrists so tight I couldn't move . . .) as I pushed back the covers that first time and, pretending not to know he was there . . . pretending, with childlike blamelessness . . . with my grandmother sound asleep in the other bed . . . I got up . . . and began walking . . . slowly, toward the window . . . pretending I knew nothing . . . as I turned my face directly into the thick black binoculars that were peering at me like two gigantic gleaming eyes as he stood on the other side of the night in his satin robe with a satin scarf around his neck . . . peering . . . and why did I think he was peering at me all the time? — because I had the childish notion then that it was my lower lip . . . and why did I think it was my lower lip? — because I was still a child with the kind of lower lip that had always gotten a lot of attention because it was the kind of thick full lower lip that looked exactly like a tiny little behind, complete with a tiny little crease down the center with two tiny little puffy cheeks on either side, and I believed, because of the way he'd always stare at it . . . the way he could never take his eyes away from it . . . that this was what it was about me that so captured this great man and this brought on an ecstatic burst of joy, a burst of wild thrilling excitement at the prospect of having such a powerful weapon — my lower lip! — but at the same time I knew better too . . . in some murky way, some animal way . . . I understood that this obsession the Maestro had, an ageless man with an eleven-year-old girl . . . was more than just about my lower lip . . . and therefore I had the choice and I knew it . . . of either accepting what was wildly beginning to happen . . . or run . . . and I chose to accept . . . because for some reason it wasn't so strange to me . . . or so unthinkable . . . it was something, in fact, that might hold a wondrous promise . . . a magnificent hope, as though a whole new sun were coming up on everything as I dashed back to the night table with the little glowing lamp we never turned off between our two beds, the little lamp that my grandmother needs in the night . . . grabbed the tube of my mother's bright red lipstick that was hidden there . . . and then . . . walking slowly back toward the window . . . began smearing it on my lower lip.

nine

For my twelfth birthday Aunt Charlotte and Juliet invited me to the Academy of Music to hear von Ochsenstein conducting from the piano his great *Starry Night*, the three of us sitting in the von Ochsensteins' box in evening dresses . . . it would be the first time I was ever at the Academy of Music . . . the first time I would see the huge gas hurricane lamps leading up the redbrick steps . . . the great glass doors, the pale stone vestibule that was lit by still more enormous hurricane lamps . . . the orange tile floors, the gilded mirrored walls . . . the ushers in scarlet jackets like toy soldiers standing guard near the great red-carpeted stairs . . . the majesty . . . and pomp . . . and then . . . inside the hall itself . . . we would be sitting deep inside gold mirrored walls and thick red velvet . . . it was old Victorian Philadelphia with nothing changed . . . not a thing, not even the enormous crystal chandelier sparkling in the middle of the great painted dome that was overflowing with cherubs trailing garlands of flowers and angels with wings and lambs and baskets of tumbling roses, and how that chandelier made of thousands and thousands of crystal drops dimmed but never went completely out as we'd be ushered to our box with a thick brass rail around it with our little gilded chairs inside made of tufted thick red velvet.

∞

For weeks I had imagined all of it — from the moment I received my formal invitation I began dreaming of that evening down to the smallest detail . . . I would wear my deep blue velvet dress that had thin long sleeves, my black satin flats with little bows, my garnet ring and my grandmother's string of yellowed pearls that had belonged to her mother too . . . and that night I would wear my hair long, not in a ponytail which I was allowed to do only on the most special occasions, my father being a stickler about hair not being "messy," which to him had almost moral implications, but that night, because it was Maestro von Ochsenstein, and because my father was impressed with all of them like everybody was, he'd let me wear it down, held back on both sides with my new silver barrettes, a twelfth-birthday gift from him that had my name, *Hannah* scrawled on each one in great swooping script as I'd sit between Juliet and Charlotte Hec, the most gorgeous woman that ever lived . . . the Maestro's exquisite wife who would be smiling coolly, majestically, absorbing all the adoration that would be pouring out of every eye in the entire place . . . that night she wore a pale satin gown the color of white roses that had that slightest touch of pink, her hair pulled into a thick ballerina's knot with big sparkling diamond butterflies in her ears that she always wore on grand occassions, her gigantic diamond ring, with one big diamond butterfly sparkling on her gown like everything sparkled that night . . . *everything!*

... even the air was crackling with life and color ... and an almost unbearable excitement as *Otto von Ochsenstein!* ... bald as a grapefruit, tall and statuesque ... the golden god of music ... *Otto von Ochsenstein!* ... in black tails, a stiff white shirt and tie walked out on stage to the thunderous applause of a completely packed Academy ... an applause that didn't stop ... people standing and applauding just at the sight of him as he bowed ... then bowed again ... and then again ... this same man ... who peered into my bedroom every night through thick black binoculars ... in a satin robe with a satin scarf around his neck ... this same man ... who peered at me through his thick black binoculars every afternoon as he stood on top of the low brick wall that went all the way around their terrace while I was working in the garden with my grandmother ... this same man ... who peered through heavy black binoculars into our dining room every evening from the top of their high diving board as my grandmother and I were beginning my cello lesson ... peering into our kitchen ... peering into my bathroom ... as he flipped the tails of his cut-away up as he sat down at the huge concert grand in the center of the stage with its one black wing raised for flight ... as the entire Academy grew hushed ... the whole poised orchestra behind him ... waiting ... and with his black tails hanging over the back of the bench ... the pinkish stage lights bouncing off his long bony head ... his back suddenly stiffened ... as his fingers began flying over the keys like racehorses while at the same time he began leading the orchestra from the piano as though he had another arm . . . as I sat stunned . . . awed . . . dumbstruck . . . by the enormity of the man . . . of the evening — of the Academy of Music . . . the elegance of it — something so precious within its grand mysterious splendor — something that spoke of merit and worth and an affirmation of the soul that makes life worth living . . . it was a whole new world — a completely other world that for one spectacular moment I was allowed to see . . . a majestic world of beauty and opulence, a world of peace and order and sanity, enormous sanity . . . enormous peace and strength . . . and I wanted this kind of strength . . . this kind of order, this kind of sanity and peace . . . a child can't know how cruel her mother is until she leaves her mother's house and sees there are other mothers, other houses, other worlds . . . as a hunger began in me that night for a different life.

ten

But trouble came when my mother found out that I had been invited not only to the concert in the von Ochsensteins' box but also to the gala at the von Oschensteins' home afterward . . . a gala evening with fascinating people . . . luminaries from the world of music, art . . . movie stars, socialites, writers and famous ballerinas which was what my mother lived for — dreamed of . . . wanted above all things — parties! *excitement!* — remarkable people to be conquered — clothes, wild drinking, sex and madness as I caught her steaming open the invitation that Aunt Charlotte and Juliet had sent . . . shamelessly, as she stood reading it over the steaming tea kettle in the kitchen — no apologies, no embarrassment at being caught red-handed . . . that was my mother, she did what she pleased — no interest in right or wrong, no interest in anyone except herself, no interest in their rights or their privacy, it was all just one big blur of what she wanted as she turned from the still steaming tea kettle and grabbed me by the arm like she was a human clamp, held me there a minute . . . and then . . . glaring at me until her eyes began to look like two hot worlds of terror and need as they kept growing bigger and bigger, and in a voice thickened with so much craving that she was almost gasping she told me as she tightened her grip that I had to *insist!* that Charlotte Hec invite her too, and not only to the concert in their box at the Academy, but I had to *insist!* that

Charlotte Hec invite her to the gala afterward — *"be adamant!"* my mother whispered as she was clutching the opened invitation in one hand and my arm in the other — "don't take no for an answer!" she ordered as she kept glaring into me with such steely intensity that it felt like her eyes were scorching two huge holes into my school blouse, and when I told her to leave me out of it — to get her own ticket as I tried to wiggle my arm away, she snapped back furiously that that wasn't the *point, dummy!* as she tightened her grip on me even more . . . which was why she always reminded me of one of those snakes that squeeze and destroy in a blink . . . but exactly what kind — a python — an anaconda — which of the great constrictors that coils its body so tightly around its victim that within less than a minute the victim is dead . . . (or maybe she was the female cobra . . . this fixation I've always had with reptiles that probably dates back to her) as she kept tightening her grip even more ferociously as she spewed out that she *knew* she could get her own ticket like she *knew* she could get my "dull as dishwater father, Leonard Gold" (she always used his entire name), not to go with her that night — to stay home so she could be *wildly free! — unencumbered! — out of the range of his rigid, tyrannical eye* . . . but that wouldn't get her into the *gala afterward* — or into their *home!* — or into their *life! — that's where I come in!* she whispered — *"get it?"* she glared at me as she flicked me on the side of my head with her thumb and middle finger like you'd flick off a bug . . . and I have to say she had a heavy hand . . . extremely heavy . . . if she was the one who was combing my hair it always hurt, never when my grandmother combed it or when my father did . . . if I had a cut, she was the one who always used tincture of iodine, which could really sting when she could have used Mercurochrome, which didn't sting at all; my grandmother never used tincture of iodine and neither did my father, as she'd smile, the sides of her lips curling when she'd see me wince from the iodine . . . which made me feel sometimes that she hated me — from time to time this was my suspicion — and if that was so, more was the pity for both of us because human beings are supposed to love their children and children are supposed to love their mothers so this flaw would make both of us aliens . . . something other than human as I'd stare at her thinking maybe she was more like one of those viper snakes with a venom in their saliva that's so powerful that once bitten the victim dies in seconds . . . "so? — yes or no? — do I have your solemn word that you will approach Charlotte Hec?" she whispered — "well? — *Well ?*" . . . and what's more she had a mania for ruining everything; it was a kind of knack she had, something in her nature . . . like at the very last minute not letting me go to a party that I had been so excited about that for days I couldn't sleep . . . her reason, either I was "fresh three months before," or . . . "on second thought," the reason was because of who might be there, because according to Kosi Gold all the boys I knew and most of the girls, with the exception of Juliet von Ochsenstein, were either "wild! sluts!" or they were "anti-Semites!" . . . (then why did she send me to a Catholic school . . . was it because the von Ochsensteins sent Juliet — was it because my father, a Jew, said that the Catholic Church was the last great stronghold of ethics and morality and that its schools, in particular Saint Theresa's were still the great bastions of excellence and discipline which he said was why Saint Theresa's was purported to be one of the best schools in the city . . . or was it because my Jewish mother was herself a full-blown Jew hater exactly like the cruelest nuns she entrusted me too — probably . . . and what's more it was always at the last minute that she dealt her most murderous blow . . . and never with any warning (something like the great southwestern rattlesnake) . . . like once being sent to my room and told to stay there all weekend for something I had done four months before, so I had a feeling that if I didn't do what she asked I'd probably be forbidden, sorry! to go, not only to the concert with the von Ochsensteins, but to the gala afterward . . . she'd say it was because I had gotten a bad mark on a Latin test last year and finally had to be punished for it like it or not as she pulled me by the arm into the living room still holding the steamed open invitation in her hand — sat down on the sofa . . . still holding me by the arm, crossed her legs and began nervously swinging the top leg back and forth very fast which was always the position she assumed immediately before she lost her temper and went wild with rage . . .

"well?" she said as she jerked my arm, "yes or no? — will you or won't you do what I'm asking you? — *yes or No?*" she was almost screaming . . . and so . . . because in the first place I was a dutiful daughter who was so filled with a fear of her — terror almost . . . and guilt . . . and pity for her too, something like that, something sentimental because she was my mother . . . and because in those days I saw her mostly as annoying — nothing more, not yet as a raving psychopath with a raging sense of entitlement that scared everybody almost from the first instant they laid eyes on her, nobody knew quite what it was — at least not at first, that made them run because people ran from Kosi Gold . . . instinctively . . . maybe they sensed her insatiable need to turn everyone into her slave — make them do all her dirty work, scratch her back, run unpleasant errands . . . make a dreaded phone call, only nobody understood this at first — they couldn't quite name or label what it was about her that made them take off instantly because she hid her lust with such diabolical skill that it took them a while to figure out that that's what it was — *yes!* — *her lust!* — her pure sheer animal greed that needed to grab, take and secure *everything for herself* as she slid along the ground like a hungry boa constrictor (which was why I secretly called her "Snakey-Laroo") waiting to squeeze whatever she could get out of any little creature that ran across her path . . . (except in my deepest heart I was sure she was a female cobra — my lifelong obsession with the female cobra who runs from her young as soon as she sees them beginning to hatch for fear of eating them) . . . *yes! — that's right! — certain snakes will eat their own!* — so, to shut her up and get back my arm and ensure that I would get to the concert and then to the gala afterward I finally said okay! — okay! I would ask Aunt Charlotte because this was my lot so I said okay like I always said okay . . . okay! I'd ask Aunt Charlotte — okay! I said — okay! okay! — and I would have too, that is — I honestly had every intention of doing it except something happened . . . something remarkable that made the Maestro become my hero because it was because of him that this miracle occurred . . . when the hideous moment arrived and I was faced with the preposterous and humiliating task of asking Aunt Charlotte to invite my mother not only to the concert at the Academy of Music but also to the gala afterward, instead of saying what I was supposed to say . . . instead of uttering even a single word . . . a strange peacefulness came over me . . . a completely new kind of calm coupled with a huge dose of unusual courage I never knew I had that had all to do with the Maestro . . . that had all to do with the way he held me by my shoulders that afternoon and told me *not to be ashamed — to never cower — to never cringe,* he said, *because what I had is what everything in the universe hungers for* . . . and this jolt of confidence gave me a brave new daring . . . a whole new flaming spirit . . . this and the way he kept peering at me through those binoculars night after night after night . . . the way he'd peer at me through those binoculars when I was in the garden working with my grandmother . . . the way he'd peer at me from their high diving board with both hands on the binoculars when I was in the kitchen with Ida Jenks . . . or appear suddenly on our side of the hedges . . . peering into our dining room as my grandmother and I were beginning my cello lesson . . . or maybe it was just the simple flush of excitement on his face whenever he'd catch a glimpse of me with Juliet . . . the way he'd stop dead in his tracks when he'd see me in their house . . . the way his face lit up . . . the excitement . . . the happiness . . . he loved me . . . which gave me a whole new kind of strength . . . that made me tough and cocky . . . and very full of myself . . . so full of myself that I suddenly had the nerve to say nothing to Aunt Charlotte when I had the chance — to just shut up . . . and then . . . without a drop of compunction . . . to tell Snakey-Laroo . . . with the coolness of a completely heartless criminal . . . that Aunt Charlotte flatly refused to invite her . . . *no!* she said . . . to the concert . . . to the gala afterward . . . *and for that matter to anything — ever!* I announced . . . surprising myself by my newfound boldness that eased me then and there into full criminality as I watched without blinking, in fact I might have even yawned as my mother became incensed . . . wild with rage . . . a rage that turned into a lifelong hatred of Charlotte Hec and my connection to all of them . . . but there was nothing she could do . . . it was too late because she didn't know a thing about the Maestro and his binoculars

. . . or about the promise now that was always in the air . . . or about the secret covenant between us . . . or about my erotic lower lip that I smeared with her bright red lipstick . . . and how powerfully it worked . . . our life in front of the windows every night was becoming the kind of eyeful that any peeping tom can only hope to catch glimpses of . . . so how could she forbid me to do anything anymore . . . or ruin anything for me ever again . . . it was over . . . because she was over . . . because now, thanks to Maestro Otto von Ochsenstein . . . I was *free!*

eleven

Where was the shame . . . or any embarrassment . . . even that first time . . . I was so shameless . . . so filled with so much unharnessed wildness — so bold . . . maybe it was just simply being twelve years old — maybe it's the age that brings with it an almost incomprehensible absence of restraint, a vulgar wildness that borders on complete depravity with absolutely no embarrassment . . . or maybe it was all the hormones that began pushing me . . . or maybe it was the nuns who filled me with so much fear and humiliation that I became hardened into something just short of complete defiance, just short of complete delinquency . . . or maybe it was the oppressive influence on my spirits of Snakey-Laroo and the Doctor, those strange creatures known as my parents who in those days had no meaning except as obstacles I couldn't begin to even fathom . . . I was already too far beyond their reach like I was beyond the reach of all the nuns, the police, the army, the navy and everyone in between . . . then no one could touch me in a way that could make even the slightest difference because of this new soaring wildness that had me flying so high — a madness almost, almost delinquency as I began doing bizarrely dangerous things like not wearing underpants to school in the hope that in class Sister Clara who was teaching math would look up my skirt while I was sitting at my desk, see my vizzy and throw me out of Saint Theresa's because I never wanted to be there anyhow — that kind of shameless insanity because to wear a starched white shirt, a maroon necktie, a short gray pleated skirt, high white socks, blue-and-white saddle shoes and no underpants to a Catholic school was tantamount to the most abject criminal behavior, and why? — because Otto von Ochsenstein, the great composer, conductor and world-famous pianist took up all the space, every inch, every molecule, so wildly in love with him . . . so madly passionately in love . . . and being in love like that amounts to an unfathomable freedom . . . a kind of freedom beyond all reason, a freedom beyond all morals or judgments . . . in fact, maybe it's the only freedom there really is . . . as school began to bear down too hard on me, all the nuns beginning to bear down too hard . . . homework and then practicing the cello too hard — what I wanted was to be with him in the woods with the trees and the grass where there was a stream behind the Narberth train station . . . and with Juliet too . . . and with her mother because I was wildly in love with her — madly, passionately in love with Charlotte Hec because she was part of him and I was in love with anything that had to do with him . . . everything that had to do with him . . . as a frenzied drive toward him began mushrooming . . . a mad hungry need to see him all the time — bump into him — catch him — run into him . . . kept pushing me farther and farther into a dark and boundless netherworld where nothing and no one existed anymore except this man . . . and in his shadow, me trailing after him . . . me, this little crumb he pulled out of the trash bin, shook off, and then . . . as if by magic turned her into a sparkling little dark-haired godlette whom he kept peering at through his heavy black binoculars night and day . . . day and night . . . creating so much madness . . . so much chaos . . . so much wild hope . . . that ushered in a whole new secret life of unimaginable dreams and wishes . . . until, finally . . . instead of going to school I'd crouch behind that high green wall of privit hedge that separated our houses . . . all day sometimes . . . *waiting* . . . my heart pounding . . . as I kept . . . *waiting* . . . to catch a glimpse of him getting into his long black limousine with Crump holding open the door . . . instead of going to school . . . hiding in the huge rhododendrons under their living room window . . . *waiting* . . . almost unable to breathe from the excitement of . . . *waiting* . . . to catch a glimpse of him coming out on their terrace in the middle of the morning . . . my dangerous behavior accelerating as I began cutting school to brazenly hang around in the shadows of their upstairs hall . . . *waiting* . . . to see him coming out of his cork-walled music room — out of their bedroom . . . coming up the stairs in one of his satin dressing gowns . . . or after school . . . lying on Juliet's bed . . . *waiting* . . . for him to walk into her bedroom unannounced, and he always did, he always walked into her bedroom unannounced . . . *waiting* . . . for him to come out on the lawn when Juliet and I were out there lying in the hammock, and he always came . . .

sitting at their dining room table next to Juliet in a state of delirious exhilaration . . . *waiting* . . . for him to stride in . . . huge, fierce and hairless, then watching him sit down at the head of that long glass table in one of his satin dressing gowns with a brightly colored satin scarf around his neck, fold his arms across his chest and begin glaring at me . . . while I sat there . . . wild with excitement . . . *waiting* . . . for night to come . . . *waiting* . . . for him to appear at the window with his black binoculars that were aimed at my bedroom like two torpedoes . . . until there was nothing except the waiting . . . no friends . . . no school . . . no cooking with Ida Jenks in the evening or sitting in the kitchen with her while I did my homework or gardening with my grandmother . . . or practicing the cello with her which I used to love so much like I used to love to hear her play Debussy or Bach before our lessons began; it was she to whom I owed so much because it was she who gave me the cello . . . she who taught me how to play when I was still too small to barely hold the bow as I'd sit on her lap with that precious instrument between both our knees, her cello, made by the great Dutch cello maker Heinrich Jacobs which stood in the corner of our dining room my whole life that she played every afternoon while I played my little quarter-size beside her, always to her right, right next to her . . . as she watched and listened and understood from the very beginning how mesmerized I was, even then, even when I was so young by the deep heartbreaking sound of even just the scales as I watched that wondrous instrument close to her body with her head bent forward, her eyes closed and that look on her face as she was playing . . . all that over now . . . done . . . swallowed up by that tall white giant, pale and terrifying in his enormity as I boldly pulled out my ponytail that first time . . . where was any shame . . . or even the slightest trace of embarrassment . . . and with my grandmother sleeping in the bed beside me . . . I pulled back the covers . . . fluffed my hair with my fingers so it fell just right . . . and then, slowly . . . knowing the whole time that a new colossal power was developing in me . . . an enormous new allure . . . and learning day by day how to use it . . . this wild horse I was trying to rein in . . . and at the same time . . . working on a brand-new kind of duplicity, something completely insincere that I was also trying to develop . . . a striking new dishonesty that the few friends my mother had were beginning to notice — my "charm" they called it . . . and trying at the same time to develop a kind of illusiveness to go with it — a certain distancing, a certain unwillingness to attach . . . or more simply put, a newly cultivated kind of haughtiness I was trying to perfect that I was sure was the secret . . . all these different personalities I was trying on like you'd try on hats as I smeared my mother's bright red lipstick all across my lower lip . . . my powerful secret weapon lip! — this thing I had . . . this little golden bullet that from as far back as I could remember everyone always wanted to kiss because as I've said, my lower lip was like a puffy little tough behind complete with a perfect little crease down the center and two little puffy cheeks on either side, and this, from the very beginning was what I thought it was . . . this was what I thought the fascination was for him . . . this was what I thought drove this man so wild that he couldn't live without seeing it for two straight days in a row . . . as I rubbed my lips together to spread the lipstick evenly the way I'd watch my mother do . . . and still acting the whole time like I didn't have a clue that the great conductor was peering at me with all his strength . . . pretending the whole time that I didn't notice his black glassy eyes glaring across the night like big blacksearch lights . . . I began my brazen little strut . . . where was any embarrassment . . . or shame . . . as I began prancing around my bedroom as I was swinging my behind like I imagined all those little starlets did in all those countless movie magazines that had become my newest textbooks . . . not Latin anymore, or French or biology, but as many movie magazines as I could carry without causing any suspicion like *Stage Door* and *Flick* which had pictures of all those little goddesses in their tight white see-through tops — their short skimpy little skirts and black shiny high-heeled shoes with black seams down the backs of their long black fishnet legs . . . all those little honeypots I wanted to emulate — copy — to excite him even more . . . my eyes the whole time . . . sneaking glances at the window that by now wasn't so much a window anymore but some kind of strange night creature that could almost talk . . . some kind of eerie "other" in our secret covenant . . . sometimes with its mouth wide open . . . sometimes with its mouth half shut . . . but always, you might say, one with me, the Maestro and his black binoculars . . . as I kept prancing around my bedroom . . . strutting and swinging my behind . . . and then . . . suddenly . . . swept by an impulse . . . standing directly in front of the window . . . in full view of those big black high-powered eyes . . . I began to slowly unbutton my pajama top . . . and then . . . with my pajama top open all the way down the front . . . I lifted my hair . . . as I began turning . . . all the way around . . . as I was thinking . . . *never be ashamed of this beauty . . . never cringe . . . never cower, because whether you know it or not,* he whispered that afternoon . . . *it's what everything in the universe hungers for.*

twelve

As the excitement began mounting . . . every night the momentum gaining . . . and without imagining or having any idea where it all was going . . . I'd pull back my covers the next night . . . and the night after that . . . and get out of bed . . . pretending each time that I didn't have a clue that the great conductor was peering at me with all his might . . . as I began walking toward the window . . . and then, standing in full view of his big black glassy eyes, I'd slowly bend over to open it . . . letting a thin slice of cool night air roll in like breath . . . and, still standing in full view of his big black glassy eyes . . . I'd begin unbuttoning my pajama top . . . and with my grandmother sleeping in the other bed, that kind of madness, that kind of sheer insanity . . . I'd let my pajama top drop to the floor while I was listening the whole time to the vulgar danger of her heavy breathing . . . as I began undoing my pajama pants . . . and then . . . letting them drop too . . . I slowly lifted my hair . . . as I stepped out of my pajama pants . . . as he kept watching . . . his binoculars in both hands like an army field general . . . as my grandmother kept snoring softly in the other bed . . . making the excitement of what was going on even more excruciating.

thirteen

My grandmother hid under her bed while she was dying, it was hard to get her out . . . my mother never mourned; all she said was that she dreamed about my grandmother every night as she cleared out her dresser and her closet, leaving me for the first time the legacy of my own room . . . which suddenly made the excitement of night boundless.

fourteen

On the Fourth of July Aunt Charlotte threw another one of her great gala celebrations exactly like the one I had been invited to on my twelfth birthday . . . only this time the occasion was to honor the Maestro who had just become an American citizen, which made the whole event even more elaborate . . . even more spectacular; parties were Aunt Charlotte's secret language . . . her way of saying everything . . . as sparkling lanterns were strung across all the trees that night with big white tents pitched out on the grass on huge silver poles, their sides rolled up so that they looked like little castles . . . and between the two great copper beech trees an enormous dance floor painted like the ceiling of the Academy of Music with the same angels and lambs and cherubs trailing garlands of flowers with big overflowing baskets of yellow roses everywhere . . . and bands of Russian violinists in Cossack costumes serenading sad old men in white dinner jackets with gorgeous women in long pale gowns . . . and the delirious way the women smelled . . . their luscious perfume mingling with the soft warm night . . . and in thinking back, in remembering all those nights, all of them . . . how they all seemed somehow outside of life — isolated . . . like night wasn't simply "night time," but rather . . . it was something that had somehow been magically transformed into yet another luxury for only the luckiest and the most magnificent . . . and as the music began, an emotional Maestro, grabbing his concert master, Anton Hobart, a tall lanky giant with deeply sunken cheeks and soft white hair, the same size as the Maestro, as the two men began to waltz, tears streaming down Anton Hobart's face . . . the high point of the evening had been earlier when the orchestra presented the Maestro with a pair of ruby, diamond and sapphire cuff links, the colors of the American flag amid tears and hugs . . . as the Maestro abandoned Anton Hobart and began dancing with his harpist, the great Sonia Lundgrin, the two of them spinning out into the warm summer night as all the guests began forming a big circle around the dance floor to watch the Maestro twirling round and round . . . next with his first oboist, the famous Eliaz Lowenberg — then with his timpanist, Sookie Grace, then with his drunken-genius flautist, the great Henry Sinclair as the Maestro's face became flushed as he began laughing uproariously as the two men were waltzing and dipping . . . then dancing with his first cellist, the world-renowned Stella Bernstein whom he held very close as he gazed at her . . . then with all his violinists, one after the other after the other — the men . . . the women . . . then with all the horns, then all the woodwinds as Juliet and I watched from our little table near the high green privet hedge . . . both of us in long white summer dresses . . . I with a great smear of bright red lipstick . . . thicker and wider on my lower lip . . . my hair down, in my mother's high white patent-leather wedgies, dripping fake pearl bracelets, a big fake ruby ring, a three-strand fake pearl choker, long fake pearls in my ears and no underwear — nothing! . . . as a tribute to my secret covenant with the Maestro . . . my legs crossed at the knee so that a lot of thigh was showing as I sat there in my newly cultivated bored and disgusted pose pretending to be as removed and as detached as Juliet as we sipped champagne and shot filthy looks of contempt and revulsion at all the guests . . . until it happened . . . what I was half dreading all evening . . . first with an earth-shaking *"p-s-s-s-st"* coming from the hedges . . . *Kosi Gold!* . . . as I shot up . . . and pretending not to hear or see . . . grabbing Juliet . . . we made a dash for the farthest copper beech tree on the far side of the dance floor . . . rushing to get to it . . . rushing to get as far from her and from her *"p-s-s-s-ts"* . . . rushing to get to where she couldn't reach or touch or lasso me . . . as we sidled up to the far side of the farthest tree . . . and crouching there, stifling peels of laughter . . . we were safe . . . finally . . . where she couldn't see us imitating her . . . and then doubling over in gales of convulsive laughter . . . and even more . . . from this new spot I could observe the Maestro perfectly as he was dancing with Aunt Charlotte . . . from this new spot I could watch him as much as I wanted and for as long as I wanted because now nothing was obstructing my view, now I was so close that I could see every look on his pale hairless face — the way he was smiling . . . exactly who he was smiling at because I was so close now, or so it seemed, that I was almost dancing with him myself . . . so close, and yet so incalculably distanced . . . so inconsolably distanced . . . as he and Charlotte Hec were twirling and spinning as he gazed at her as one would gaze at a goddess as they were doing fantastic dips, he lifting her high into the air as she clung to him, her arms around his neck in worshipful adoration . . . she had everything — yes . . . first of all she had Otto von Ochsenstein, who was much more than just a man — he was worlds — whole galaxies . . . she had unimaginable beauty, she had wealth . . . she was a famous ballerina with all the grace and drama . . . still rail thin and as white as chalk, both of them pale and colorless as though they were made of clouds . . . that night she was wearing a long green gown with real gardenias across one shoulder, her pitch-black hair pulled back into her usual ballerina's knot with real gardenias fixed around the knot like jewels . . . as I watched the Maestro kissing her as they were spinning and dipping . . . then watching as the Maestro's brother, the famous portrait painter Sir Oscar von Ochsenstein grabbing her out of the Maestro's arms and began dancing with her . . . pressing her even closer than the Maestro had as he gazed at her even more adoringly — yes . . . she had everything . . . *everything!* . . . that's what I was thinking as I watched the Maestro dancing with his sister Marta, the one with the dyed black hair . . . then with his sister Tania with the dyed red hair, both of them like two great turkey vultures with their wings spread wide as they were all dipping and twirling . . . then watching him dancing with his secretary Gazelle Dimitri-Corson . . . then with his second cellist, Ludwig

Rozinski, watching everyone laughing as the Maestro and Rozinski, their arms wide open as they began almost marching around each other with their widespread arms, doing little tricky motions with their feet, some kind of Russian folk dance they both knew . . . watching the circle around the dance floor begin to break as everyone began dancing . . . watching the Maestro looking for Juliet . . . finding us on the far side of the farthest copper beech tree . . . bowing to his daughter in a great flourishing gesture that requested she dance with him . . . watching as she walked with her father across the grass . . . he smiling . . . Juliet removed, disdainful . . . barely looking at him . . . the Maestro returning Juliet to the huge old copper beech tree and then bowing to me with the same great flourishing gesture . . . people watching as we walked across the grass . . . his whole enormous body trembling as we began to dance, and as he held me close . . . I felt something hard pressing against me — maybe his wallet . . . maybe a private object from his desk that he carried for good luck . . . who knows — maybe it was food . . . maybe a piece of fruit — a banana or an apple . . . I didn't know, while out of the tail of my eye . . . without looking directly over there . . . just sliding a sidelong glance in the direction of the hedge . . . my mother . . . now on the von Ochsensteins' side . . . in a long black evening gown.

fifteen

Late that night, the Maestro, in a long satin dressing gown that was open all the way down the front . . . began peering into my bedroom through those heavy black binoculars . . . only this time he was holding them — not with both hands like he always did . . . but with only one . . . while in his other . . . he was holding an enormous and terrible piece of his body . . . as I got out of bed . . . and began walking . . . slowly . . . toward the window.

"Ahead — always think that way! Ahead — Not behind."

OTTO VON OCHSENSTEIN

part two

sixteen

It started with a fever, something struck with such force that I collapsed on the playground at school and was immediately rushed to the small local hospital . . . then, in the bleary daze that followed, the weeks in bed, so sick my father stopped working to sit in the little blue chair in my bedroom across from me, sleeping every night in the bed that was once my grandmother's — his open unblinking eyes staring at me every time I looked over . . . through all those days of wracking chills crossed by raging fevers, it was my father . . . say what you want — too strict! — too prudish! — too rigid! — too stern! — it was he who was always covering me, giving me sips of water, pills, drops . . . opening the window, closing the window . . . as visions . . . wild, colorful . . . mystic and magnificent, the overflow of something deeply understood . . . something known beyond knowing . . . as my father and Saint Theresa — *my Saint Theresa!* — *my beloved treasure* — she wasn't cruel like the other nuns — oh no, *never!* . . . not my Saint Theresa of Avila — the *real* Saint Theresa of Avila who was beautiful and brave as she was telling me to be kind to my mother, that that was the most I could do on this earth . . . to just be kind, which is all conversion is she said . . . to love with your whole heart and leave the rest to Luck because Luck is God . . . and yes, it was time for me to convert she said . . . from this day on to change and become a real *duende* woman just like her, flamenco in the highest sense she said as she kept stroking my head and kissing me and blowing her hot breath on my cheeks as she was whispering about *a huge and sacred scheme, something holy and magnificent . . . where I could go if I were loving enough . . . kind enough, especially to my mother — I couldn't make fun of her anymore or laugh at her or make jokes about her or talk bad about her to anyone if I wanted to become a duende woman with a real flamenco soul because a real flamenco soul is kind — and kindness is the best we can do, the most we can give, the most there is on earth . . . kindness, which is all conversion is,* she kept whispering . . . as I was becoming more and more lost in trying to hear her . . . hear her voice . . . voices whispering . . . so many whispering voices . . . about if I wanted to go to this sacred place *I had to love with my whole soul and leave the rest to Luck . . . because God is Luck . . . remember this . . . love with your whole soul and leave the rest to Luck* her hot fiery breath was echoing as an ecstatic peace was filling me as Jesus, Buddha, God, Moses and Mr. Engelburg who had the dark little drugstore on the corner near the Narberth train station with his gray little dog that looked like a mop were all joking around with the Four Horsemen of the Apocalypse whose picture was hanging in my father's waiting room . . . until I wasn't able to untangle myself from all their voices . . . so many voices . . . or from their heat . . . or from the smell of their horses . . . or from the smell of Saint Theresa's long black habit that had the same earth smell as my grandmother while my body was being consumed by the fires that created them . . . as I began slipping . . . slipping . . . right to the edge . . . then Saint Theresa pulling me back . . . again . . . and then again . . . and this was how it went . . . Jesus appearing now and then . . . Brown hovering over my bed as a sort of fat brown cloud with enormous seering eyes as he kept whispering to my grandmother that I should love with my whole soul and leave the rest to Luck because God is Luck as my grandmother kept smiling as she was sitting in the little blue chair beside my bed holding her cello as though she were about to play as she was telling Brown how good I was — a born musician she was saying — better than she ever was she was beaming proudly as Saint Theresa kept kissing me with her hot fiery lips . . . the heat of her hot breath on my cheeks as she wrapped me in the black folds of her habit as though her habit were a shroud as all of them began swirling round and round . . . round and round they all were going . . . Brown and my grandmother and the Four Horsemen of the Apocalypse . . . Mr. Engelberg and Saint Theresa . . . all of them going round and round like the carousel in the park as they were beginning to all get smaller . . . and smaller . . . smaller . . . and smaller and smaller . . . no, don't go . . . don't leave . . . *I'll do better* . . . I'll turn over a brand new leaf — you'll see I was shouting — I'll be kind — I'll love with all my heart and leave the rest to Luck I promise as I was trying to grab the folds of Saint Theresa's thin black gossamer habit . . . as the bleary daze began to lift . . . as though waking from a dream . . . reality slowly coming back . . . reality slowly growing bigger and bigger . . . reality finally filling all my senses as I began looking around my room as I laid in my pillows . . . looking at all my familiar belongings . . . my pale blue wallpaper with the little circles of yellow flowers, my desk, my desk chair, all my dolls, my stuffed bears, my bureau — my bookshelf with my scrapbooks . . . my corkboard on the wall above my desk covered with pictures of movie stars . . . Doris Day, Rita Hayworth . . . my windows across with their organdy curtains, stiff and gray from neglect with the window shades half drawn . . . looking at my windows as memory was easing in . , . slowly limping back . . . staring at my windows . . . then at the windows of his music room across the afternoon that were black, all their windows — black . . . their whole house, black . . . no one there . . . he was gone . . . the house was empty . . . dead . . . night after night . . . "where are they?" I asked my father, "the orchestra has been on tour almost from the day you became sick — pneumonia," he said, "in both lungs," — "and Juliet?" — "she went with them, her mother too — all of them," my father said . . . so he was gone — everyone was gone . . . everything . . . gone . . . as I looked over at my father sitting in the little blue chair across from me reading the paper with his glasses on his nose . . . my mother peeking to ask how I felt, a handkerchief across her mouth so she wouldn't catch what I had which wasn't contagious anyhow; we were never friends, my mother and I, but near the end of her life she was able to tell me that she was sorry about the fact that she never had much love for me . . . she was born that way she said, with no maternal feelings, it wasn't my fault she said, that she could never feel what she was supposed to feel which made her feel like a monster, but she was an artist she said — what kind of artist she didn't know, just that she was an artist and needed to be free to live the life of an artist whether she knew what kind or not . . . watching her eating cherries in front of my bedroom door, watching her spitting the stones on the floor, smiling as she was eating them . . . smiling as she was spitting the stones on the floor . . . smiling because I wanted some and she wouldn't give me any . . . but rather than give in I began hating cherries . . . *never her!* . . . she was my mother and even though she had a nasty streak I wanted to do better . . . be kinder . . . love her with my whole heart and leave the rest to Luck . . . that was my honest intention as the days rolled on, and as the days rolled on I kept trying . . . playing gin with my father in the evenings, he always letting me win which enraged me . . but I didn't say anything because I was trying to do better — be better — be kinder . . . trying to love him with my whole heart . . . trying to become a *duende* woman with a real flamenco soul like Saint Theresa . . . thinking that maybe one day I would become a nun . . . do good things . . . help people . . . devote my life to prayer . . . to God . . . sleeping sometimes all day, reading movie magazines, doing my schoolwork and gazing at their windows that were dead . . . and then . . . the announcement by our housekeeper Ida Jenks . . . that I had visitors, Juliet and the great conductor were coming up.

seventeen

In the ecstasy of their return the little fiend went back to being the little fiend . . . no promises kept, no conversion . . . nothing changed, no new leaf . . . as my mother's bright red lipstick was smeared on in a hurry, thicker and wider on my lower lip . . . my hair pulled loose, all my fake jewelry grabbed and smacked everywhere, my hands with all my junky rings and bracelets trembling . . . and as Juliet and I were hugging . . . my eyes were riveted to the Maestro — the towering hairless golden god of music — Otto von Ochsenstein, standing in the doorway of my bedroom glaring at me with that same pale fire blazing in his thick reptilian eyes as he came toward my bed and took my hand . . . and that night . . . weak and trembling . . . I went to the window . . . his satin dressing gown, open all the way down the front as he was holding his black binoculars with one hand . . . and in his other . . . that monster piece of his body . . . as he kept peering at me . . . as our terrible secret life began again.

eighteen

He came the following day and the day after that . . . and every night . . . weak, exhausted and drenched in perspiration I went to the window . . . and every night . . . letting my pajamas drop to the floor — first the top . . . then the bottom . . . with his finger upward and spinning I'd turn . . . with his finger pointing downward I'd turn and bend . . . then more signals as he'd motion me to sit on my little wooden desk chair . . . then crossing my legs . . . then uncrossing them . . . then spreading them wide apart . . . then spreading them wider apart as he'd begin doing something to the monster in his hand, exactly what, I didn't understand . . . while he kept peering at me . . . peering . . . peering . . . and then, still peering at me, the binoculars suddenly disappeared as he slumped for a moment and then disappeared into the blackness all around him until the next afternoon when, like nothing happened — like the whole earth hadn't trembled for that one flashing moment the night before . . . he arrived in my bedroom with a huge bouquet of roses that Ida Jenks put in a vase . . . with chocolate candy . . . with chocolate-chip cookies he was munching as he came in, completely mindless of what anybody might have thought — my father, his daughter, Aunt Charlotte — even Ida Jenks, who knew everything the way that servants always know . . . as our secret covenant continued . . . night after night . . . the promise between us growing day by day — my mother insinuating herself the minute he arrived as though she were part of the secret . . . part of the promise that now was always in the air . . . and even though he paid no attention to her . . . even though he acted as though she weren't in the room as he expounded on the wonders of the orchestra's tour of Florence! — Rome! — Venice! . . . the concerts . . . the audiences and their colossal success as he pulled the little blue chair up close to my bed as he was telling me all of this as he took my hand, and then . . . "how conversations like these have magical powers," he smiled, "souls touch — spirits embrace," he murmured as he kissed my hand as he gazed at me . . . as my mother sat rigidly on the other bed, each time in a different getup . . . each time her dyed pitch-black hair slicked back with heavy goo and too much makeup on . . . each time her long dagger fingernails filed and polished to perfection . . . each time, certain in her mind as she sat there pursing her lips and smiling that his daily visits, flagrant and preposterous as they were — shameless and outrageous . . . had everything to do with her, in her mind I was only the excuse.

nineteen

At the end of summer there was another great gala event at the von Ochsensteins and that's when it happened . . . something the Maestro called "taking our vows" . . . again, the party was under a stupendous net of colossal stars — again, the same wandering band of Russian violinists in the same Cossack costumes, the same yellow roses . . . the same little tables out on the grass with the same long white organdy skirts . . . the same magnificent dance floor between the two great copper beech trees painted like the ceiling of the Academy of Music with champagne being passed on the same silver trays to the same old men in white dinner jackets with the same gorgeous women with the same heavy smell of perfume everywhere . . . all of it the same . . . exactly . . . except this time Snakey-Laroo and the Doctor were asked to come in a half-baked attempt by the Maestro to avoid trouble, and it worked . . . they were both wildly flattered . . . wildly overjoyed to be invited by the great golden god of music — Otto von Ochsenstein, their neighbor and now their friend, and more, that night my father became the Maestro's personal physician, another brilliant maneuver by von Ochsenstein that turned even my father — even that taciturn old stoic with his bushy gray eyebrows and extremely quiet voice who never bowed to anyone — even he was turned that night into a big giggling lick as my mother kept shooting the Maestro spicy glances, pursing her moist red lips and rolling her eyes as if to say that she and Maestro von Ochsenstein were the only ones who understood what the story really was; that night I was wearing the same long white summer dress I wore to all the von Ochsenstein parties with the same mountain of fake jewelry . . . bright red lipstick and no underwear! — not anymore as I snuck into their house searching for the Maestro . . . not a soul was in there . . . no one! which fascinated me . . . that ghostlike quality a house takes on when there's no one in it that's almost a distortion, something dreamlike because theirs was never empty . . . there were always people . . . except on two occasions, that night and the day after Christmas a year later . . . otherwise, the big white house on the other side of the hedges was always bustling . . . noisy, filled with musicians, staff — maids, movie stars, writers, the cook, the chauffeur, ballet dancers, hangers-on and all the dogs . . . but that night . . . the only sound was the distant sound of a party going on outside somewhere out on the grass — the distant sound of maids in the kitchen mingling with the far-off clanging sounds of dishes . . . and the even more distant sound of music coming from a terrace somewhere in the night . . . all of it seeming so far away that for a moment the emptiness of that enormous place made me feel the same sweeping loneliness I felt when I was very young listening to my parents' parties going on downstairs . . . this was what I was thinking as I stopped on the landing and was leaning over the banister, my hands on the brass railing that wound round and round all the way down that great white swirling fan of stairs that were narrow at the banister and then fanned out . . . and this fascinated me too . . . I was mesmerized . . . I couldn't take my eyes away even though I remember becoming dizzy by looking down . . . dizzy by the great swirl of marble stairs that looked like a gigantic Chinese fan . . . dizzy by the immense brass banister that kept winding round and round like a swirling golden ribbon . . . as an indescribably painful filling up suddenly overwhelmed me . . . something so heavy and big entering me from behind . . . and then bearing down so hard inside . . . that for a moment it felt like I was having all the life crushed out of me . . . as the Maestro . . . with one hand on my shoulder . . . and the other holding onto the banister as he was whispering . . . "now . . . at last — now," he was murmuring . . . "you are my secret little wife," he whispered . . . and then made a terrible little sound as he slumped onto me.

twenty

And that's how it began, that August when I was twelve . . . my murky journey as his secret little wife.

During the week the orchestra held rehearsals every afternoon. Behind the stage was a small room called the Maestro's Chamber . . . a dreary little place with no windows, a piano and a piano bench, a huge purple sofa — a desk and a desk chair and an enormous photograph of the composer and conductor Musil Mosolovitch, the Maestro's idol . . . and every afternoon after school, my job was to bring the Maestro lunch . . . have a rushed and steamy little conjugal visit and then leave so he could take a nap.

The job of bringing Maestro von Ochsenstein lunch was traditionally reserved for the most gifted students of various members of the orchestra . . . it was always an honor, always a privilege for exceptional young stars to have the opportunity of spending time with Maestro von Ochsenstein discussing the fine points of their instrument or the pieces they were studying; in my case however it was a sham . . . a complete charade the Maestro insisted on by saying that I was not only an extremely talented cellist (which he didn't have any knowledge of — nobody did — not then) but more important, he said I was his daughter's closest friend, and in this case, and as a personal favor to his entire family, implying that by the orchestra making this concession on his behalf a rift would be healed between the Maestro and Juliet . . . and since Maestro Otto von Ochsenstein was not only the golden god of music almost everywhere in the world, within his own city and especially within his own orchestra it was so profound that he could insist on anything . . . even that I be paid the usual five dollars a week for the five days of work I was expected to perform, and even get it.

Mostly the Maestro wanted crab claws or a crab cake for lunch with an ice cold Coke and usually the Maestro invited his daughter, but the invitations were always trickery — dishonest ingenuity to make it appear that those luncheon invitations were the act of a good father doing everything to make things right with a disgruntled daughter . . . except that it was more than a disgruntled daughter — Juliet hated her father, despised him . . . her conviction was that nothing mattered to him except music, and this conviction and her accompanying contempt for his "supreme egotism" as she put it gave us all the privacy we needed — her rage at him and her refusal to come to lunch was his freedom and he knew it and he used it . . . and as implausible as it might sound . . . he seemed to not only not care how enraged she was . . . it seemed to amuse him . . . but what about me — where was my conscience — my pride — where was any loyalty to my dearest friend — where was some concern for how she felt . . . what was happening to me . . . that's what I didn't understand — who I was turning into . . . and once she even came — twelve years old, quiet, glowering, intensely angry unattractive Juliet with her thin pale hair, dead white powdery skin like his, her big hawk nose and thick pale eyes the same as her fathers, a perfect replica of this person she despised as she sat there rigidly while the Maestro stood up, and staring blandly off into space began pontificating about the works of the painter Alice Neel — the importance of rest for one's ability to be creative . . . and finally (and disastrously) . . . a little speech about *the soul of the artist!* which was a familiar prelude to a pompous lecture on music . . . its power . . . its magic . . . which was the one subject that so enraged Juliet that she'd run and he knew it . . . so if he said this intentionally . . . or if it was more a mistake than deliberate, her father still exquisitely played the rift between them like he played everything . . . exploited everything — used everything for his own indomitable needs — in this case trumping up the appearance of an act of infinite goodwill . . . and yet intentionally or not . . . throwing in the one thing that would make Juliet wild with rage, until it all became some kind of thickly plotted fiction, all of it — some fantastical kind of opera without the music . . . making the business of a cover-up tragic art.

twenty-one

And this went on for almost a year . . . after school every day the Maestro's long black Chrysler limousine, after Juliet refused any further luncheon invitations, would drop her and Anna Marie Vaccaro off . . . then Crump and I would continue on into the city to the Sansom Street Oyster House, pick up the Maestro's crab cake and then continue on to the Academy of Music where Crump dropped me, the crab cake and the Coke at the musicians' entrance while Crump waited in the limousine the hour or so until I came out . . . then Crump, who knew what was going on like our housekeeper Ida Jenks knew what was going on, the way that servants always know what's going on . . . that strange jury who see and hear everything but never let on . . . would drive me, now the Maestro's secret little wife . . . sitting in the back of the Maestro's long black Chrysler limousine to my house to report to Snakey-Laroo and the Doctor at dinner that night how things were going at school . . . with my cello lessons that I was taking now with George Kirchik, a former student of my grandmother's as well as a teacher at the famous Curtis Institute . . . and my "job" with Maestro von Ochsenstein as I'd race upstairs the instant dinner was over . . . do my homework . . . run back downstairs to practice when no one was in the dining room . . . then run back upstairs . . . and start . . . *waiting . . . waiting . . .* until midnight . . . sometimes later . . . for the great conductor to appear on the other side

of the night in his satin dressing gown and binoculars
. . . and when he appeared, whenever he appeared . . .
I'd begin my little dance . . . first slowly taking off
my pajama top . . . then my pajama pants . . . then
climbing up on the seat of my desk chair that was now
always in front of the window . . . always also waiting
. . . and holding on to the back of the chair with my
back to him . . . I'd slowly bend over . . . as he'd begin
his business with that monster in his hand . . . then he'd
slouch forward — disappear . . . I'd put my pajamas
back on . . . do the rest of my homework and go to
sleep . . . the nights and days somersaulting out of each
other like little Chinese acrobats until the weekend when
Juliet and I would go rolling down the huge white snowy
hills behind Saint Theresa's over and over ourselves . . .
laughing . . . laughing . . . hurling snowballs at a long
line of cedar trees named for all the nuns we hated and
then laughing so hard we'd fall backward into the snow
still laughing . . . movies on Saturday afternoon, Juliet
and I at the Egyptian Theater with its orange and gray
wooden pyramids — its green and yellow sphinxes
and funny lettering that looked like daggers that were
supposed to be Egyptian — the dry wood smell of the
penny-candy store across the street — the new thrill of
jukebox music . . . my delinquent behavior peaking as
I began hooking school more and more to sit on the
Narberth train station platform and stare at the almost
surreal beauty . . . a whole wild teaming universe in
there of brightly glaring flowers . . . waves of enormous

butterflies . . . birds darting . . . vines with huge white morning glory blossoms climbing up a telephone pole as I'd sit in ecstatic bliss . . . listening . . . to the sound of the flowers . . . to the sound of the vines . . . to the sound of the birds that were going mad with joy . . . as if all of life all at once were bursting out of an eggshell . . . because the famous conductor and composer, Otto von Ochsenstein was always beckoning . . . smiling . . . luring me . . . out into the garden in the early evening . . . up into an upstairs bathroom when no one was around . . . onto the apron over the stairs . . . over to my bedroom window . . . *there!* . . . every time I'd turn around . . . *there!* . . . with every breath I took . . . *there!* . . . *always there* so that now there was always a soaring happiness — always a wild excitement that kept growing . . . by his constant presence . . . by his constant smile . . . by the way he was always looking for me . . . the way he was always calling for me from the bottom of their stairs when I was upstairs with Juliet . . . the way he was always teasing me when people were around . . . joking with me . . . baiting me and now constantly swatting me on the backside . . . so that as unbelievable . . . as unimaginable as it was . . . as preposterous as it seemed — it appeared that the world-renowned pianist, composer and conductor of the famous Philadelphia Philharmonic . . . Maestro Otto von Ochsenstein was in love with me the same as I was in love with him . . . although he never said a word about it — not ever once.

twenty-two

Then one day, out of the blue, Maestro von Ochsenstein (or "Otty," as he was called by everyone except I never could, to me he was always either "Maestro" or "Maestro von Ochsenstein," no matter how intimate or how intense the moments were that I called out his name) . . . told my father that my "gift" warranted my studying *"the cello much more strenuously"* — then he told my father that I had to stop taking lessons with my teacher at Saint Theresa's and with Mr. Kirchik at Curtis Institute because I was to have an audition the following morning with the renowned Stella Bernstein, the first chair of the Philadelphia Philharmonic because according to Maestro von Ochsenstein there was something to be said for accomplishment — even fame, and what's more he said, he liked having geniuses around him even if he had to create them himself.

I was twelve at the time and by then I had been studying cello for seven years — first with my grandmother — then for credit at Saint Theresa's with Sister Madeline Morrison and after my grandmother died with George Kirchik at Curtis Institute, but with all the studying I was still very much in my own world, a world that didn't include the slightest ambition or drive to accomplish anything — all I wanted then (if I wanted anything) was to be free . . . to watch the flowers . . . hook school whenever I pleased, sit in train stations . . . go into the woods behind Saint Theresa's and listen to the birds — because to me school had always been despicable so more instruction of any kind was only more oppression . . . and as for the cello, it was something I just did — like walking or taking a bath, and if, like my mother said, I was "overly attached to a piece of wood," it was because I had been overly attached to my grandmother, whom I started studying with on my little quarter-size when I was five — this astonishing musician, a musician who had been on the concert stage before she was thirteen . . . so for me it wasn't unusual to have such a teacher because this teacher was my grandmother and her genius was all I ever knew . . . and as for her — my grandmother, she played not only until she lost her hearing, but long after, as deaf as a stone she kept practicing all her unaccompanied Bach suites — her unaccompanied Britten, the Walton and the Dvořák, so much, so diligently and so often . . . besides everything else she played all the time, that that rich deep gloomy sound . . . like the sound of an old man moaning at the bottom of the sea . . . like ghosts, or dead people coming down with the rain into a garden in the night . . . things like that that I imagined as a child that were always in my ears . . . even in my sleep . . . and in my eyes . . . I could even hear her music just by looking at that gorgeous instrument leaning in its corner in the dining room . . . that treasure that was given to her by the great Czech cellist Oskar Stigl . . . and although she never appeared on the concert stage again, she gave lessons to people who did — her students coming in the late afternoon for all the years she still could hear and when she became completely deaf, it was I . . . I was her last student, so for both of us the cello did the hearing . . . and the speaking, responding to the slightest touch and then saying everything in its own gloomy way as it finally became all things to her . . . and to me . . . her ears that worked so I didn't have to be resentful and so bitterly ashamed that she couldn't hear . . . it became her dark voice — my precious childhood toy, almost a person you might say — a woman without a head as well as a place to go . . . I was her last student and from the beginning the one she had the most ambitions for — but the more I turned to playing, the more it became a place to hide . . . a cave . . . a dark hole to climb into . . . but always usual . . . always awash in all its shining ordinariness . . . in its familiar everydayness with nothing special about it in any way because it had always been there like my great teacher had always been there . . . something we just did . . . and did together . . . that I knew how to make a certain melancholy sound make sense of everything was a way of life for me, it's what I had always depended on to get through, but ambition was never part of it . . . ambition had nothing to do with what the cello meant to me . . . so it came as a shock when Maestro von Ochsenstein insisted *I become more strenuous about my art!* (what art? — what did that mean)? . . . *that now I must commit myself to the cello so completely — so absolutely — "so totally that we will have whole new horizons — new worlds with exciting new conversations that will bind our souls,"* he whispered as I was sitting on his naked lap doing my homework . . . "ah, there's so much you don't yet understand," he'd laugh . . . we were in his music room on the second floor sitting in his green velvet chair . . . I in my school uniform . . . he stark naked — hairless and as white as marble as he was whispering . . . "ah, so much I have to teach you . . . so much I have to make you know . . . and not with your head . . . but with your *soul!*" he was whispering as he was playing with my knee . . . and even though I wasn't sure I knew what he was talking about . . . and even though I was sorry to be leaving Sister Madeline at Saint Theresa's . . . and Mr. Kirchik . . . and even though I didn't understand about *"new worlds and new horizons"* . . . I would have done anything . . . taken any kind of lessons . . . acrobatic lessons . . . cello lessons . . . Polish lessons . . . trombone lessons . . . any language the Maestro spoke I would have learned to speak because I wanted him to love me . . . so much . . . that I could have become anything.

twenty-three

After my audition lessons were arranged with the renowned Stella Bernstein — first at her little redbrick Federal on Rittenhouse Street every Saturday morning at ten . . . and then inevitably, the Maestro arranged with Madam Bernstein to have my lessons given at the Academy while he was taking his "little nap" so that *riding home he could discuss with me the subtle affect of the cello on the entire orchestra* — he wanted me to know these things because according to Madam Bernstein . . . I had "an enormous gift" . . . was a *"natural"* . . . who was very, *very* well trained and from a very early age, she told the Maestro that afternoon when he came to pick me up . . . "look, even just in the way she puts the bow to the strings," she whispered to him . . . and even though I didn't understand their enthusiasm . . . or believe what they were saying — to me it felt like they were talking about someone I didn't know — some strange "other" whom I had no connection to . . . something happened anyhow . . . this ordinary thing I did all the time — the cello that was so usual . . . so common a part of my life — suddenly leaped out of its hiding place to become something else . . . something entirely different . . . suddenly something important . . . even magical — in fact, maybe the only magic in my life there ever was . . . as I promised the Maestro on the ride home that afternoon that I would work hard with Madam

Bernstein — very hard I said . . . as he whispered as he began undoing the zipper of his pants . . . " all you need is a cello and a bow and you can have the stars."

twenty-four

She must have been in her mid-forties when I met her, and yet to me then, she seemed ancient in some ageless awful way . . . something old and finished about her unlike my grandmother or Charlotte Hec; they too were old to a girl not yet thirteen, but they were vibrant, alive . . . all in color; Madam Bernstein, however, had something dead about her, something almost rank — she was sloppy and loose with sharp staring eyes hiding an enormous curiosity . . . limp thin long brown hair, usually dirty — a lined face with slightly bucked teeth — she spoke with a lisp and wore strange things like big floral shifts and thick suede sandals with no polish on her toenails as though the last thing in the world she registered or could even begin to fathom was how she looked, and from the instant I looked at her, I knew she knew . . . everything! just in the way she eyed me, the coolly impersonal way she'd speak to me, even in the way she began teaching, nothing friendly, as though there were some thick invisible line she wouldn't cross — an icy professionalism she hid behind because now I was the secret little wife . . . and she knew and respected it . . . Stella Bernstein had been a startlingly brilliant prodigy, appearing on the concert stage at fourteen, strong, stern — magnificent . . . and from the first instant I laid eyes on her, I knew, in exactly that same way she knew . . . that once long ago something went on between the Maestro and her . . . as I got the eerie feeling . . . scary almost . . . as I was standing there that the Maestro might have had a lot of secret little wives . . . and with all his secret little wives he probably created a lot of flaming geniuses . . . because he liked geniuses, like he liked crab cakes and ice-cold Cokes . . . and later . . . much later, I learned that I was right . . . that it was she, the then young and astonishingly brilliant Stella Bernstein with whom he was caught sleeping an hour before his marriage to Charlotte Hec.

"Talent is not enough — without total commitment you are Nothing!"

OTTO VON OCHSENSTEIN

part three

twenty-five

Every year the Philadelphia Philharmonic went to Lyon to perform for one week at the ancient Cathedral of Saint Sebastian which was ninety miles south of Paris, then up to Paris for another week of concerts at the Cathedral of Notre Dame, and that year, the year I turned thirteen, I was invited to join Juliet . . . who invited me or why was never clear — I didn't know, but Juliet and I were ecstatic at the prospect of being together, and I was even more ecstatic at the prospect of being out of school for an extra week.

When the Maestro traveled he traveled with a huge entourage composed of his three sons from his previous marriage, their fiancées, his brother the famous portrait painter Sir Oscar von Ochsenstein, the Maestro's ancient mother and her companion, the formidable Sylvia Ostroff — both his turkey vulture–looking sisters with all their wigs and capes — his cook, his driver Crump, his secretary Gazelle Dimitri-Corson, his staff, all the dogs, all the maids — the entire orchestra without their spouses, and on this trip, instead of my father, a certain Doctor Leopold Epstein became the Maestro's personal physician, my father having been replaced — no longer even the Maestro's friend . . . the Maestro was like that — dropping people, discarding them without a word — then once they were gone the door was slammed on them and he never looked back; in this case the eruption occurred because Maestro von Ochsenstein wouldn't allow my mother to join my father even though my father and I were part of the entourage, the Maestro being famous for his unwillingness to bear the company of anyone who bored him — he had the idea that he was a kind of lonely Don Quixote who waged a constant and solitary war against an invisible concept he called *The Vulture! — The Monster! — The Beast that feasts on Everything! — Endlessly! Destroying Everything! Boredom!* — The most horrifying element — More horrifying than the most deadly disease because it's a living *Death! — a Scourge! —* an *Abomination!* and as such he wouldn't tolerate a boring cook in their home, a boring maid, a boring driver, a boring butler or even a boring dog — anything that Maestro von Ochsenstein had any contact with could not bore him — *Period!* . . . my father took my mother's side, my mother screaming at me that I couldn't go out of loyalty to her; there was a vicious squabble with me storming out of the house in boiling tears, then a phone call from Madam Bernstein saying in her calm and rigid voice that I was scheduled to play the day after Easter in a chamber ensemble in the ancient cathedral of Saint Sebastian; it would be a great honor for me she said, because I would be performing for the first time in public with such esteemed musicians as Aaron Sorkin, Philip Stern, Gerald Wolf and herself, and although my mother still vehemently forbade my going, screaming that she was still the boss in this family and therefore she would "do the deciding" while she continued shouting obscenities into the phone, my father said that of course I would go which left my mother insane with rage — crazed! . . . if my father was afraid of his wife as most men are — or if my father was afraid of my mother like everyone who knew her was because she was out of her mind . . . in this particular instance it didn't show.

twenty-six

We sailed on the SS *Constitution* to Nice — then up to Lyon in our own private train . . . before the trip I was carefully instructed by the Maestro to be on my guard at all times — no touching, no staring, no private looks of any kind or anything that would give any indication to anyone about our "secret marriage" because his mother, the ancient Polish countess Anka Koslowski von Ochsenstein would be watching the Maestro like a hawk — therefore, I was to give him a pair of my panties to carry in his pocket before we sailed, unwashed . . . was that clear? — then when we got on the train for Lyon, another unwashed pair . . . of course my cello lessons were to continue with Madam Bernstein daily as well as all our daily homework assignments to be done "down to the letter" . . . those were the rules! . . . and as the ship pulled slowly out of the harbor like a slow gigantic birth . . . as the crowds on the peer began to grow smaller . . . recede farther into the distance until finally all that remained were little dots . . . the farther from the dock we moved, the more sullen the Maestro became — colder and more distant . . . as I began to sense in him . . . like I sensed things in a flash in those days . . . with a completely other knowing . . . with a mute clear other eye that came from being the kind of child who saw . . . everything! — nothing escaped me, maybe because of the nuns and always having to read between the lines with them — *live* between the lines . . . or maybe it was having the kind of mother where I never knew where the next blow was coming from and therefore I had to always be on my toes which made for another kind of intelligence . . . a wary kind of intuitiveness . . . Einstein said that intuition should account for only ten percent of knowing, but with me it counted for everything, it was my armor as I stared at the Maestro realizing as I was staring how much he hated his family . . . not just Juliet but all of them . . . how he got icy and quick-tempered when they came up to him and began talking, especially if any were cheerful and enthusiastic, which not only repelled him but made him instantly infuriated because he was so completely disinterested in all of them — had no compassion for any of them — no sympathy, no kindness; he didn't care about them in the least because they didn't interest him . . . all there was was a kind of molten rage at the sight of them . . . who knows why the bubble always bursts with Maestro von Ochsenstein, but sooner or later it always does; this time it happened as soon as the ship silently cut through the late afternoon heading for the open sea like some gigantic monster, some enormous warrior dragon surrounded everywhere by death . . . "how simple it would be — how easy — to just step off," he whispered as he peered over the railing into the swirling huge gray depths . . . as Juliet and I sat in the lounge doing our schoolwork, she writing poetry more than studying while I not only practiced at least two hours every day but toiled over every drop of each assignment because for me nothing came easy; I had to work for everything and always harder than the others because I was the only "Jew" in school that year, and therefore, because I was so completely alone I was filled with even more fear of all those horrifying women dressed all in black who'd glare *"Kike"* — *"Mockey"* — *"Christ Killer,"* every time I spoke or asked a question or passed them in the hall . . . they hated me . . . simply because I existed . . . and nothing would change it, which is what I had to wrestle with and finally what I had to accept, but it took a toll . . . as Juliet and I would get all dressed up at night with lipstick, high heels, mountains of fake jewelry and then sneak down to tourist class to smoke cigarettes and lie, speak in fake accents, tell wild stories about who we were, who our parents were — my fake father was Al Jolson and Juliet's, Mario Lanza — or we'd tell them we were Russian gymnasts or princesses from Albania as we became more and more delinquent . . . drinking gin, smoking constantly and lying to everyone to hide the longing . . . to cover the sense of being completely cut off . . . from the hills behind our school . . . from the Egyptian Theater . . . from the train station platform where life was so peaceful and so magnificent . . . and for me, most of all from the Maestro who seemed to have become someone else, a stranger . . . odd, how what you expect to be so unimaginably wonderful, a fairy tale almost, never is, never can be . . . it isn't possible because the whole other side is completely left out . . . the struggle side, the terrible lonely frightened side — I was thirteen years old and filled with so much sorrow because of the harrowing way I missed Snakey-Laroo . . . my grandmother, our housekeeper Ida Jenks and my father as I sobbed into my pillow every night . . . every night in our luxury state room, which was all glossy burled wood with round glass portholes and thick blue carpets I cried myself to sleep . . . while outside the air was black, the sea choppy, terrifying . . . as I kept hearing all of them calling me to come down for dinner . . . what I loved the most they all were shouting up from the bottom of the stairs — *"Lamb Chops!"* they were yelling up to me . . . only I couldn't answer them, not any of them — not anymore.

twenty-seven

In the Hotel Ville Florentine in Lyon I had the only fight I ever had with Juliet . . . something about a blouse she accused me of taking without asking first and no apology would stop her, she just kept going and the worst part was, I was living in the same room with her, packed for the whole two-week trip so close to her that it felt like I almost couldn't breathe . . . maybe I took her blouse without asking — maybe I didn't . . . I couldn't swear to anything because in those days I was always in a fog . . . a kind of mist clouding my senses as I trudged over to Madam Bernstein's room every morning, my lessons continuing like clockwork . . . and with them the bewilderment of rarely seeing the Maestro who had become remote, distant . . . on board ship when I was in his company, which wasn't very often, I couldn't talk to him — dare even look at him, not even for a minute because his family was always around — his sons, one of his son's fiancées — his mother and her companion always looming . . . they say that longing is the better part of happiness — Goethe says it makes for the purest joy, especially if it's for something you can never have but it didn't seem that way to me . . . on board ship I was homesick all the time . . . on land it was fighting with Juliet over a blouse . . . on land it was Juliet becoming unmanageable — it was practicing three hours every day after a grueling lesson with Madam Bernstein and still not seeing the Maestro, never seeing the Maestro

. . . and since the music still meant nothing to me — since I still wasn't stirred by it — since it was still the familiarity of the pieces that I loved, not the music itself, it was all becoming some kind of joyless exercise, some prescribed thing I was required to do . . . nothing like the happy days with my grandmother or my happy music lessons with Sister Madeline at Saint Theresa's which was the only thing at Saint Theresa's I cared about as something gloomy was taking over and the harder I worked the worse it got until even the opportunity of studying with the great Stella Bernstein was becoming a grind . . . if I had a gift (which I always doubted anyhow), it was a modest gift, nothing spectacular . . . I had been tricked into believing it was something more, I had been tricked by so much flattery, tricked by so much wild praise and from such enormous people like the great von Ochsenstein himself, and from the renowned, world-famous Madam Stella Bernstein so I worked — really worked . . . taken in by all of it — tricked . . . until it was becoming a whole other story, a whole other life I didn't ask for, understand — or want . . . I was lost in what seemed like a huge glass forest with no way back as I kept practicing . . . taking lessons . . . practicing . . . practicing . . . taking lessons and practicing . . . until, on one of those mornings . . . in Madam Bernstein's suite in the hotel . . . suddenly he arrived, the great bald giant of music — Maestro Otto von Ochsenstein — as our lesson abruptly stopped — everything stopping abruptly — life itself coming to a screeching halt as he sat down and crossed his long spidery praying mantis legs in gray slacks and a gray tweed jacket with a brightly colored satin scarf — green I think, around his neck . . . as Madam Bernstein asked me to play all three unaccompanied Britten suites for him . . . and as I began, flustered and trembling even though I knew each one of those suites so well but it was the first time I had been with him since we came away and the first time ever that I was asked to play for him as I listened to Bernstein telling him almost as though she were speaking to herself, "this child's uncanny ability to understand what she's playing" . . . her eyes on my fingers as she was speaking . . . "her uncanny ability to hear the music," she said, "it's as though she's listening, not with her ears, but with those eyes," she whispered to the Maestro as though she were still speaking to herself . . . and as I looked over at Maestro von Ochsenstein as I began playing the first Britten suite . . . I caught in that fraction of an instant a strange broken look . . . an almost begging look — a terrible pleading look that changed his whole face as he was staring at my fingers on the strings . . . as he suddenly got up . . . and began walking toward me . . . his thick blue reptilian eyes filled with tears as he took my grandmother's cello out of my arms, leaned it against the wall — then took the bow . . . then he raised me out of the chair . . . and led me into the dim bedroom of Madam Bernstein's suite and closed the door . . . and as he sat down on the bed and began unzipping his pants . . . I began doing my little dance for him like I always did . . . twirling round and round as I pulled out my ponytail letting my hair fall loose as I began taking off my clothes . . . and then . . . as I bent over the pink satin chair in there with my back to him like I've bent over so many chairs . . . I began begging all the gods in heaven and under the sea to make him love me . . . want me . . . need me more than he ever did . . . and in return . . . I vowed to all those same good gods . . . that I would work even harder — practice even longer — become even better . . . because I could now . . . now I could do anything . . . because he was back.

twenty-eight

Their home in Paris was a tiny golden palace in the middle of a teaming garden mad with flowers and vines climbing over low stone walls and little gates that didn't quite close, old stone benches . . . and butterflies . . . hordes of butterflies . . . all kinds of butterflies darting in there as though they were some kind of child's toy — something on strings like puppets that were frantically darting, madly darting among all the flowers and vines behind the low stone walls making their teeming little garden into some kind of exquisite little fairyland . . . and inside it was even more astounding . . . everything was gold, white satin, marble and mirrored walls with gold leaf arches and in the middle of all the gold and white satin . . . a long black concert grand where the Maestro would play for hours every day surrounded everywhere by still more flowers . . . on every table . . . on the mantle . . . in great crystal buckets on the floor in front of both gold-leaf arches with sunlight pouring in from all the huge glass doors as the Maestro was playing his own magnificent creations, one after another after another from the moment we arrived . . . and that's when it all began . . . on an afternoon during a ferocious storm . . . because we were in Paris . . . the Maestro said he would like to hear Madam Bernstein and I play Fauré's "Allegretto Moderato" for two cellos . . . and when I backed off . . . actually ran upstairs . . . he began yelling up to me — then he tried to lure me, cajole me . . . use all kinds of supplications, even tricks and bribes to coax me down to play this tiny piece with Stella Bernstein . . . until it became so uproariously funny that everyone downstairs was laughing, roaring . . . but I was too afraid — too hideously awed and intimidated . . . *"how can you let her sit like that? . . . it's disgusting!"* my mother's voice . . . echoing . . . over the ocean, over the world — louder than all the music in the universe . . . *"it looks like she's playing with her you-know-what!"* she would shout at my father every time she saw me sit down and place the cello between my knees, even though her mother sat like that her entire life.

But wonders happen — maybe because of the terrible weather that day . . . maybe it was my fantasy that the sound of the cello was like black rain falling from the sky bringing dead people down into a garden in the night . . . maybe the rain and thunder made me miss Snakey-Laroo and the Doctor so unbearably — or maybe it was some sudden understanding of sound that made me take my ponytail out and go downstairs, . . . made me carry over my chair . . . made me sit down next to Madam Bernstein . . . made me put the rosin on my bow, and then . . . Stella Bernstein, the world-famous virtuoso and I, a dumb little thirteen-year-old in old blue jeans, Juliet's brother Oliver's big baggy sweater and my old blue sneakers . . . taking our A from the Maestro . . . we began . . . as everyone in the house came trickling into the living room . . . all the maids, the cook, the Maestro's sisters, his son Daniel . . . Daniel's fiancée,

Gay Jones . . . members of the Maestro's staff . . . the great portrait painter Sir Oscar von Ochsenstein, Aunt Charlotte, Juliet . . . all of them forming a circle around the two of us that went out into the hall as we played that tiny piece with so much hope, so much passion . . . that exquisite little gift we were giving the great conductor . . . a moment of gorgeous music like diamond dust that we were filling the whole world with . . . glittering . . . sparkling . . . dancing . . . as we played our hearts out as they all began clapping clapping clapping clapping clapping . . . and later that night . . . the Maestro, putting his napkin down in the middle of dinner, getting up from the table, walking slowly through the dining room, through both gold-leaf halls and across the living room as the soft sound of talking and laughing stopping — a hush falling over the whole house as Maestro von Ochsenstein sat down at the huge concert grand in the middle of the living room with its one black wing raised for flight . . . then calling to me in a booming voice, and at the same time beckoning me with his enormous hand . . . this time only me . . . as I got up from the table, took my cello that my grandmother brought from Prague, her treasure — my treasure now . . . and began walking . . . someone bringing the chair, his son Daniel I think . . . watching the Maestro watching me . . . as I kept walking . . . with the Maestro watching me . . . as I sat down . . . taking my A from him as he was glaring at me . . . as the family and their guests — the maids, the cook . . . everyone coming into the living room and how the music that night never happened like that again — not ever again in my life . . . not like that . . . not ever . . . not three nights before in Lyon which had been my debut, a chamber concert at the Cathedral of Saint Sebastian where the whole dark cathedral that night resounded with the heartbreaking Schubert Quintet, I playing second cello next to Madam Bernstein, the two of us sitting side by side in front of that sea of faces — first violin played by the magnificent Gerald Wolf, second violin by the majestic Aaron Sorkin . . . or a few months later on the Maestro's insistence, going to Washington to meet with the great Alfred Blik, auditioning for his master class and being accepted instantly as Maestro Blik sat in his thick black leather chair nodding his head with his fingers laced over his lips . . . of all of that nothing compared to that night in Paris in the Maestro's little golden palace as the Maestro and I began playing the Fauré Serenade . . . the thrill of playing alone with him for the first time mixed with the awe I had for this great man, this great composer and conductor Otto von Ochsenstein — the passion I had for him — the excitement . . . making that night the zenith of my whole life . . . a night that nothing has ever compared to since . . . not even my first guest appearance at the Academy of Music a few months later with von Ochsenstein conducting the magnificent Philadelphia Philharmonic, then maybe the greatest symphony orchestra in the world . . . even that didn't compare to our thrilling little concert in that little golden palace playing the Fauré Serenade . . . just the two of us as I kept praying that now he'd never be able to do without me . . . now, he'd love me more than he ever loved anyone . . . now, with the success of the evening exploding all around us he'd love me more than he ever dreamed he could ever love . . . as the joy of hitting every note exactly right . . . the wild exuberance . . . the Maestro's enormous pride and excitement as he threw back his head and roared with laughter as we both stood up . . . he kissing my hand and beaming wildly as he held it high in the air as everyone kept clapping clapping clapping clapping clapping clapping as we bowed . . . then bowed again . . . and then again to all the clapping clapping clapping . . . for the triumph . . . the spontaneity . . . the danger . . . the risks . . . the courage it took as I emerged from my little hole — that dark place the cello used to mean . . . as he suddenly let go of my hand, turned his back to me and sat back down at the piano and began playing Chopsticks as he tried singing to it . . . then some old Parisian melodies, one after another after another as he began whining through his nose like Piaf . . . then *La Marseillaise* with everybody singing with him, their glasses raised as the Maestro stood up at the piano with his glass raised to all the guests as he proposed a toast to the great French composer Gabriel Fauré . . . and still with his back to me he proposed another toast — this time to Paris as he melted back into all their adoration . . . back into their wide open arms and smiles and laughing . . . my moment with him done . . . gone . . . like an ephemeral bubble that bursts at its peak in midair . . . as he was holding up his glass as he proclaimed that he was Parisian! . . . that Paris was his true and only home . . . that only here could he live! — breathe! — make love! . . . eat! . . . real omelets! . . . real vanilla ice cream! . . . real cheese . . . announcing that this glorious city made any trace of sorrow in him disappear as he told everyone gathered around the piano that night that it was here that his exquisite childhood was spent in the most aristocratic circles . . . as he began toasting his past with tears coming to his thick reptilian eyes as he spoke of the lavishness of it . . . the beauty, the grandeur as though our gorgeous little concert never happened . . . as though a door slammed shut that I didn't understand — that I would never understand . . . as I sat down beside Juliet on the white satin sofa and stared at her . . . as he continued toasting his ancient childhood home as he looked over at the old countess Anka Koslowski von Ochsenstein who glanced up at him from under her eyebrows without expression . . . their servants . . . their art . . . the jewels . . . the private tutors and liveried chauffeured limousines as the list went on and on as he continued toasting with tears streaming down his face . . . as Juliet and I, sitting on the white satin sofa next to Juliet's brother Nicholas who was laughing as he was making cracks . . . "lies! — all lies!" Nicholas was laughing at every word that came out of the Maestro's mouth . . . "my father changes his history every time he stands up to speak," Nicholas kept laughing as he was telling everyone sitting close enough that the Maestro was one of eleven children who barely had *"enough to eat! . . . Polish peasants!"* he was laughing — *"anything* but titled . . . *anything* but aristocracy, unless you call a hovel outside of Warsaw with a chicken and a goat *Aristocracy!"* he was laughing so hard now that everyone sitting near him could hear everything . . . "so dirt-poor," he went on, "that my father began playing the organ in a local church when he was just high enough to reach the keys in order to make the few extra pennies *The Countess!* over there needed to get them through," Nicholas said, his face flushed now from laughing as he pointed to his ancient grandmother who was watching him . . . "but my father never mentions this does he — oh no — not this — this part of the ever-changing history of our great *Aristocrat* he keeps strictly to himself," Nicholas was talking loud enough now that anyone across the room could hear . . . his dark dirty secret — their poverty . . . which is a kind of shame and suffering completely unto itself as the Maestro stood up at breakfast the next day which was our last day in Paris and started tapping his glass with his knife to get everyone's attention . . . the whole entourage gathered . . . his two turkey vulture sisters, his mother, her companion, his brother — Juliet and her mother Charlotte Hec, his three sons by his former wife the famous actress Martina Mastrianni with her horrendous nest of dyed black hair . . . and with a yellow satin scarf around his neck and the same green satin dressing gown he wore when he snuck into my bedroom after our triumph the night before . . . that same green satin dressing gown he was wearing when he appeared at the side of my bed late that night as I sat up groggy with Juliet asleep not three steps away as he began staring at my lower lip as he stood there telling me to wet it . . . "wet it," he kept whispering as he opened his dressing gown, "wet it — that's right," he whispered again, "that's right, wet it," he kept whispering as he pushed down my head, "that's right," he kept whispering — *"that's right,"* he whispered as he held down my head . . . *"oh yes! . . . yes! . . . that's good! — oh! — that's good!"* he was whispering as he threw back his head . . . staggered for a second as he let out that little half screaming gasp with Juliet asleep so close to where he was standing that if she opened her eyes she would have seen *everything* — because the room was small and never completely dark . . . not really . . . with mirrors everywhere . . . that's what I was thinking as I kept staring at that same green satin dressing gown at breakfast the next morning that was slightly open all the way down the front and even though it was tied loosely around the waist it was still easy to get a look in there, get a glimpse of the thin dark shadow that clearly showed he had nothing else on . . ."today," he began, "on this, the last day of this remarkable trip," he said as he stared out over the breakfast table with that faraway look on his face . . . again, as though he were staring out over the thirty-five hundred faces that packed the Academy four nights a week, "I should like to say a few words about the word *Enough* — this most magnificent word," he smiled as Juliet and I nudged each other under the table . . . my mind wandering homeward to Snakey-Laroo and the Doctor, to Ida Jenks . . . to school, to my grandmother and to the enormous music room across the night with the big green velvet chair . . . how he'd rub his finger across my lower lip when I'd be sitting in there on his lap . . . I in my Catholic school uniform with my blue-and-white saddle shoes and white high socks as he sat naked in the chair . . . and how . . . always, just as I was about to ask him to help me with something I had to memorize for school the next day . . . he'd close his eyes as he'd take the pencil out of my hand, put my hand down there and whisper that if I would do it now exactly the way he liked . . . tight he'd say — very tight . . . as he'd hand me the jar of Ponds cold cream that he kept under the chair to lather it with . . . the chances would be good he'd say with his eyes still closed . . . that on our next trip downtown . . . I could have . . . *anything!* . . . as excitement . . . mixed with a heady sense of power made me dare to hope . . . dare to believe . . . that now . . . if I did exactly what he wanted me to do . . . exactly the way he wanted me to do it . . . he wouldn't be able to live without me . . . that he'd love me more than he ever loved anyone . . . as this crushing hope began choking me as I opened the jar . . . "because the word *Enough*" he was smiling as he stood looming over the breakfast table in his dressing gown, which was always slightly open down the front with a yellow satin scarf around his neck . . . sometimes he looked like funny things to me . . . that morning it was a completely colorless white giraffe . . . an albino you might say . . . or was it a green satin Gila monster? — I wasn't sure as I'd squint very hard because I was told that if you squint you always see the truth . . . "because the word *Enough* cuts both ways," he said . . . "first, to be able to say I have *Enough!* — to be able to say Thank You as I put my hand across my heart — *Enough money!* — *Enough food!* — *Enough warmth!* — *Enough* — *Yes!* I whisper in humble gratitude as I bow my head . . . a simple statement," he smiled, "a simple feeling, but in so saying . . . I begin my long and noble march toward *freedom!* . . . *Enough!*" the Maestro proclaimed as I looked over at Nicholas who was leaning all the way back on the two back legs of his chair, a soft straw hat with a thick navy band down over his forehead with his eyes half closed, laughing. . ."or perhaps," the Maestro smiled as he looked around the whole enormous breakfast table as I was wondering if that morning he didn't look more like a huge white crocodile . . . one of those very old ones that eventually lose all their color and become a kind of a permanent gray . . . but chillingly . . . with advancing age . . . their sense of smell increases . . . until they can smell a snack as far as five miles away . . . or I was thinking maybe he was the famous albino crocodile from the Amazon in a green satin dressing gown with a yellow scarf around his neck standing straight up on his immensely powerful tail that can swat down a hippo and then eat it whole in less than two minutes, that incredible monster devil with its insatiable appetite — its lusts and never-ending hungers with its thick pink albino lizard eyes — "that's it!" he was shouting, "by God I've had *Enough! — Enough abuse! — Enough torture! — Enough mistreatment!* — No More shall I abide!" he said as he put up both his hands as though to protect his breast from some imaginary adversary, and in so doing his robe opened a little more, showing yet more of the heavy laden darkness under it . . . "and last but not least," he seethed as he glared at his mother . . . "what one gets — *Madam!* . . . what one is given — or what one never gets — *Madam!*" he was glaring at her as she was munching serenely on a piece of buttered roll . . . "and since there is no making up for what one never gets — *Madam!* " he was glowering as she smiled at him indifferently as she kept munching — "again the word *Enough* must be struggled with . . . grappled with to assess with accuracy . . . with cold — honest — brutal accuracy, we must finally ask ourselves . . . in spite of all . . . in spite of everything — have I *Enough*? And if I can answer *Yes!* If I can utter this mighty resounding *Yes, I have Enough! — If I can say these words . . . Then I can also say, 'I'm Free!'*" the Maestro was almost whispering as he lowered his long hairless head and bowed . . . his arms across his chest as his green satin robe opened even more . . . showing even more of the shadowy darkness in there as everyone at the table began clapping modestly — if there was a rift between Juliet and me because of her blouse it was over completely by the time we were home; by then everything was back to normal which meant the same gales of laughter, secrets, smoking cigarettes and whispering as my lessons resumed with Madam Bernstein after I delivered the Maestro's lunch, put on my little show as I pulled out my ponytail as he began unzipping his pants . . . back to our Saturday afternoon shopping jaunts — me, the Maestro and sometimes even Juliet . . . my trip one Sunday every month to Washington for my private lesson with the great Alfred Blik, followed by his grueling master class . . . meeting a cellist from Maryland — tall and thin with messy soft brown hair who kept staring at me, never saying anything, just staring who made hideous bowel movements in every bathroom at the conservatory and to whom I might have even been drawn — I who was never interested in "boys," only interesting men like our American history teacher at Saint Theresa's, Father Raymond O'Malley . . . or possibly the great Alfred Blik himself — yes . . . my confusion with Maestro Blik . . . wondering why he never made a pass, never made a move, not that I cared, only that I wondered why there was never so much as even a hint . . . never so much as even a look — nothing — not even the faintest smile; it was always the music, only the music, until I began to feel like there was something wrong with me . . . something lacking because he treated me as a musician, not as a woman, and I was a woman; I was thirteen . . . and on the trip had gotten that first great drop of blood . . . that heralded the coming of my time.

"The real trick in life is to know how strong you are."

OTTO VON OCHSENSTEIN

part four

twenty-nine

It happened the day after Christmas . . . The von Ochsensteins' house was empty — not a soul, even the cook, Mrs. Stillwaters who was always in there somewhere was gone that day; it was one of those freezing December afternoons, no sun . . . all the trees were stripped, their bare branches shaking in the wind like bones . . . the ground had gray snow piled everywhere — even the air that afternoon was a penetrating kind of gray gunmetal as we ran from the train station to Juliet's house, too cold to even talk, too cold for even the best of spirits to survive outdoors . . . but it was even worse inside . . . infinitely worse . . . because it was we who discovered her — Juliet and I.

That day the entire family was at a party out on the Main Line given by a member of the board of directors of the orchestra, a socialite who gave the same eggnog party for the same crowd on the same afternoon after Christmas every year, year after year, only that year — the year we were both thirteen, instead of going Juliet spent the day with me, first in my room smoking cigarettes, then both of us went to the home of one of the girls in our class, Dickey Shannon . . . danced a little, smoked more cigarettes . . . then at about four we headed back to Juliet's house because at her house, unlike at mine there was always food . . . it had been snowing on and off all day so instead of going in through the front door we went around back to the butler's pantry because there was a small courtyard back there with a closed-in entrance to the back door where we could take off our boots . . . and that's when we first sensed something . . . all five dogs were outside in the courtyard with snow on their fur, kind of aimlessly looking at us . . . then . . . as Juliet began fidgeting in her pocket for her key, we saw that not only was the back door unlocked, but it was barely closed so that all the dogs had to do to get inside was push against it with their snouts . . . something made them stay out in the freezing air . . . almost as though they were confused . . . baffled . . . as we went in . . . went through the butler's pantry and into the kitchen . . . and saw . . . Charlotte Hec . . . hanging from a rafter in the ceiling by a long white scarf.

thirty

Strange things go through your mind, ridiculous, unrelated, almost nonsensical things in an effort to survive the horror you're looking at, for me it was about how cold my hands were even though I had on heavy gloves — that's what I was thinking as I kept rubbing them together . . . that's what kept going through my mind the whole time I was staring at Charlotte Hec in a red satin nightgown, her eyes wide open as she was hanging by the Maestro's long white satin opera scarf . . . and how after that for both of us it was a completely different life . . . a completely different world — just the emptiness of their home after Juliet's mother's suicide was something beyond the senses . . . dizzying — so vast and sweeping that being there was somehow like being lost on your own street, even for me, the interloper — the intruder . . . the great trespasser . . . and I knew, from that first instant . . . as we were standing there that afternoon bundled in our coats and gloves and hats and mufflers, that nothing would ever be the same — not ever again . . . and this knowing, like a thick red thread kept running through the terribleness of what we were looking at — this absolute knowledge . . . even for me . . . even then . . . profound and certain . . . that we were being transformed as we were standing there into entirely different beings — shrunken by a horror so enormous that our old lives were over then and there . . . finished forever . . . as we stood looking . . . numb . . . and we were to stay numbed . . . for years . . . and years . . . and years . . . and beyond the numbness was the certainty that both our lives, before that moment were now a dream — distant and remote, almost unimaginable . . . could there be life for Juliet without her mother — that is . . . if life meant a certain joyfulness — a sense of well-being — a sense of gratitude . . . in Juliet's case the answer was no; from that day on it was as though life for her was an addendum to living, something tacked on after the fact — after the continuum was over — something almost not real.

For the two days and the two nights preceding the funeral Juliet moved in with me as all the arrangements were being made, but there was no peace for her, nowhere to run, no way to shed any of it . . . she said she would never comb her hair again, never brush her teeth . . . sleeping was the only break in the agony, waking the nightmare that kept mushrooming bigger and bigger as attacks of wild despair began assailing her as we moved silently through those next two days, Juliet becoming a human ball as she lay curled, forever changed in my grandmother's bed across from mine with the window shades pulled down . . . her mother's death and the sorrow it carried was the price she paid for life — the price we all have to pay . . . but it was her mother, not mine . . . so for me it was something else . . . for me it was the despicable thought that now the coast is clear . . . for me it was the despicable hope that very soon

I'd be able to claim my spoils . . . that very soon I'd be with the Maestro forever . . . it was the knowledge that what happened to that exquisite beauty, that gorgeous bird . . . had nothing to do with me; it was fate I kept telling myself — some synchronicity of random events that build upon each other to create a nod to the gods that made this all-consuming wish become a possibility — a possibility that began creeping into everything . . . this all-consuming dream of claiming my place beside him that began fogging every waking hour as I kept reminding myself that none of it was my doing . . . a terrible event suddenly made an unimaginable hope become a possibility . . . but it wasn't my fault — none of it . . . as I kept seeing her hanging by the Maestro's long white satin opera scarf . . . her wide-open eyes . . . the long red satin nightgown she was wearing . . . her bare feet, almost misshapen from so many years of dancing — no slippers . . . no jewelry . . . no flowers in her long black hair . . . no note . . . nothing . . . except a photograph of the Maestro's brother, the famous portrait painter Sir Oscar von Ochsenstein clutched in her hand that had already become stiff from death . . . as I crept into my grandmother's bed beside Juliet and putting my arms around her began to sob . . . and sob . . . and sob . . . and sob . . . as we both lay there crying until the sun came up.

thirty-one

The funeral service was held under the enormous portrait of Charlotte Hec in the costume she wore in *Swan Lake* . . . the gigantic portrait by Sir Oscar von Ochsenstein that swamped the whole downstairs as it loomed above the orange marble fireplace in the living room, thirty times bigger than life . . . so enormous that it was almost as if it were someone unto itself . . . an overwhelming presence, like some gigantic paper doll that watched and judged, lived and breathed and hated, as Juliet and I sat on the sofa that afternoon listening to the Maestro deliver the eulogy.

At the end of eighth grade Juliet was enrolled at Garrison Hopkin Academy in New Hampshire and I left Saint Theresa's to attend the prestigious School for Professional Children in the city which for me, on the heels of all that had gone before was startling . . . just in the way the teachers smiled, the decency and respect shown to every student . . . the spirit of kindness and genuine concern in utter contrast to my life at Saint Theresa's . . . as well as to the dark life I lived outside of school . . . they say, "once in the camps, forever in the camps"; I was flustered by so much goodwill — stunned . . . I had to get used to it . . . I didn't know how to act or almost who I even was anymore because by then so much was lost . . . so much gone . . . the carefree spirit, the lightheartedness — a sense of well-being, fun — all of it was hanging from a rafter in the kitchen by a long white satin opera scarf as the whole world was beginning to cave inward with heavy black shadows beginning to fog up everything — dark glimmers of fraudulence springing up everywhere.

By then I had been making guest appearances with the Philadelphia Philharmonic for almost a year . . . for almost a year I had been appearing in front of a whole sea of faces staring at me . . . applauding me, even standing ovations as I'd stand beside the Maestro . . . as playing the cello was becoming strangely fraudulent, it was as though the better I was becoming as a musician, the more unworthy I'd feel about myself, the uglier . . . the more undeserving — a fake . . . as the Maestro and I would walk out on stage and bow . . . then bow again . . . as the vision of Charlotte Hec, her black flying hair . . . her wide open eyes . . . hanging by a long white satin opera scarf kept flashing on and off like a long row of blinking yellow traffic lights . . . as I suddenly began resenting people hearing me play . . . what business was it of theirs I'd seethe as I was staring out at all of them through half-closed eyes which the Maestro said was "only natural" after what we had seen that day . . . as I began to resent them watching me . . . as the vision of her terrible sad feet dangling in front of me kept flashing on and off . . . on and off . . . as I began longing for my grandmother; more and more I began craving her patience, her steady kindness . . . more and more I began craving the comfort once again of her little bird hands and thin little bird wings folding me into the warmth of all her silent sweetness as I began slipping back into that other place, tumbling more and more into that dark hole again where I used to hide — that safe warm home the cello used to mean when playing had nothing to do with performing because I never wanted to perform . . . I became a musician because Maestro von Ochsenstein wanted it — I became a musician because the Maestro created musicians, made geniuses out of anyone he could, he had that knack . . . and even though my grandmother had this same dream for me . . . for me playing was still about her, nothing else . . . from the time I was old enough to sit on her lap and help hold the bow with her cello between both our legs . . . that was all I ever wanted . . . just to play . . . whenever I could . . . and for as long as I could because it was something my grandmother gave me and everything my grandmother ever gave me I kept . . . everything . . . including not only her cello but her love of all the unaccompanied Bach — all her books, her pearls, her garden tools . . . her love of the Britten suites that I played after she died sometimes so late into the night that my mother would storm into the dining room in her pink see-through nightgown, livid, her hair in big pink rollers with Nivea lotion slathered all over her face so that she looked something like a birthday cake as she'd grab the cello away from me, yank me out of the chair and then furiously pull me by my arm up to my room because it enraged her to know how much I loved anything that wasn't her . . . including the wonder of that noble instrument . . . including the comfort of its somber melancholy sound — it infuriated her.

"But that was *then!* and now is *now!* and now you are a *Star!*" the Maestro glared at me. "The past is *done — over — poof!*" he said as he flicked up his enormous hands . . . (this man who never grieved — couldn't mourn . . . as though something in him was missing — the ability to suffer like he had a huge black hole in the middle of him that couldn't bleed) . . . " and what's more," he said, "you must stop looking back!" he glared, "because once you look back you're *finished — done!*" . . . "listen," he whispered as he kissed my hand, "we have a magnificent future — do you understand? — *magnificent!*" he whispered again, "you'll learn all my new works, all my glorious new compositions so we can record together . . . tour the world . . . perform in all the great music halls of Europe because by then you'll be truly remarkable . . . because you have the gift, and never be mistaken — it is a *gift!* — a priceless *gift* the gods have bestowed on you . . . you have the strength, and now with me and my new compositions *we have the future! — everything is Ahead! . . . Ahead! — not behind . . . Courage!*" he'd whisper as we walked out on stage together, he holding my hand high in the air as we bowed — then bowed again — and then again; ahead I kept telling myself . . . not behind . . . we'll record together, tour the world . . . perform in all the great music halls of Europe — I'll learn all his new work — all his great new compositions . . . become truly remarkable — not just good . . . *remarkable,* because I have a gift . . . and I have strength and now we have the future I kept telling myself as I kept telling myself that it wasn't my fault . . . none of it . . . I didn't do it . . . I didn't do anything to Charlotte Hec — *nothing!* . . . it was a terrible series of sad random events piled on top of each other that had nothing to do with me . . . *nothing!* as I took my A from the Maestro as I was gazing up at the painted dome in the ceiling at the Academy lost in daydreams, distracted . . . by a shadow cast again by those small transparent wings of hope . . . the promise of touring the world with Maestro von Ochsenstein . . . just the two of us . . . the promise of recording with him — the promise of performing all his exquisite new works and since it wasn't my fault . . . since I had nothing to do with it . . . *nothing at all — nothing!* . . . the dream of living happily ever after was beginning again to soar out of the ashes . . . was beginning again to weave its toxic promise . . . its lethal hope . . . as I was suddenly playing with renewed strength . . . with an exciting brand-new passion as I was imagining how wonderful it would be if Maestro von Ochsenstein and I . . . now that the coast was clear . . . could be married! . . . what difference I was thinking as I was wildly playing the Elgar Concerto . . . if he was fifty or sixty or seventy years old — *so what! — who cares!* . . . I was thinking as I'd seamlessly glide like a ray a week later into the Dvořák in B minor . . . imagining myself no longer Hannah Elizabeth Gold, ninth grade prodigy at the School for Professional Children . . . (the root word prodigy meaning "monster"), as we'd walk out together . . . holding hands and bowing to more and more applause . . . more standing ovations . . . even hoots and whistling . . . but rather . . . the glorious Hannah Elizabeth Gold *von Ochsenstein!* . . . winter holidays in Switzerland . . . Paris in the spring in that little golden palace that was always teeming with musicians — movie stars, artists . . . famous writers . . . only now I would be sitting at the head of every table . . . sleeping in all those enormous beds that were so huge, so imperious — so grand and magnificent in every house that nine people could comfortably sleep in any one of them but of course they wouldn't . . . it would just be me . . . eating breakfast with the Maestro every morning . . . the two of us smiling as we'd sip our coffee I'd be thinking as he'd nod to me . . . shoot me that look that sent me flying into my part of the glorious Rococo Variations . . . now with all my soul . . . with everything I had . . . because with Charlotte Hec out of the picture I'd be thinking as we'd walk out to yet more thunderous applause . . . and still more standing ovations . . . we have a future . . . that's what he said . . . as I imagined myself the stepmother of Nicholas, Oliver, Daniel and Juliet von Ochsenstein — why not I'd wonder as I'd concentrate for a moment on my fingers against the strings . . . the way the cello felt between my knees . . . the floor pin positioned perfectly as my bow kept hitting every note exactly right and I knew it as I kept shooting the Maestro glances and the Maestro knew it too and the whole packed Academy of Music knew it as the Maestro was almost dancing on the podium, his arms around the music . . . no baton . . . never a baton . . . just his enormous hands flowing like rivers . . . as the stage lights were flashing off his gleaming head as he half closed his eyes . . . with his open hands now curled inward toward his face like claws . . . and then later . . . after the concert . . . and after my little wifely duties — "*that mad magic hunger,*" as he called it . . . as he was zipping back up his pants . . . he'd pull me over into the sofa in his dreary little chamber at the Academy and start glaring at me — no smile — "now that you're a *Star*," he'd say . . . "there are a few simple rules," he'd begin . . . (always the lectures . . . moralizing, distant and superior after our sweaty escapades were over as he was tucking in his shirt) . . . "first of all," he'd say as he began buttoning it . . . (*button . . . unbutton . . . button . . . unbutton . . .* that's what I'd be thinking as I'd be pulling on my sweater *as a picture . . . of me . . . in a little yellow sundress . . . my father . . . holding me by both wrists so tight I couldn't move . . . trying to struggle free . . . trying to bite — kicking him . . .*), "you must *never* say please — you must *never* say thank-you and *never* under any circumstances apologize for *anything*— second!" he said — "never rush because *stars don't rush* — we let *them* do all the rushing! — third!" he'd glare at me, "don't be too nice! — that's very important — not to *Anyone*! — and last and most importantly . . . you must always look *Ahead*! — *think*

Ahead! — not behind!, which means that now you must concentrate on nothing but the music . . . and you must concentrate on it so absolutely, so completely, so totally that you and your instrument become one body — one voice — because one day," he said as he kissed my hand, "you will be playing *My Work — Mine!* in front of *the entire World* . . . Do you understand?" he smiled . . . and as I nodded yes . . . I understood as I was pulling up my socks . . . he pulled me down . . . again . . . with that look . . . again . . . as he began unzipping his pants!

"Ah . . . to be seventy-five again!"
OTTO VON OCHSENSTEIN

part five

thirty-two

In the months following the tragedy the most beautiful music of the Maestro's long and creative life was completed . . . his glistening *Night* for orchestra and cello — *Heartbreak* for piano and cello — *The Charlotte Concertos* which were three concertos for full orchestra and cello . . . and the magnificent *The Wolf and the Canary,* a ballet the Maestro had been working on in collaboration with the great choreographer Denko Steniskowski, about the gleaming illusions of youth and its abounding hope against the growing disillusionment that comes with age and the unbearable hopelessness that is its consequence because according to von Ochsenstein, what makes youth so astounding are all the hopes — the expectations . . . the promise . . . when in fact, life breaks your heart over and over and there are no happy endings the Maestro would laugh sardonically as he'd mark each of those exquisite works in his funny backward left-handed scrawl — *"To the beauty and to the grace of the magnificent Charlotte Hec"* . . . and in those first weeks after the tragedy, he would demand I sit with him in that barren music room . . . all night sometimes . . . demand I bring my cello and not dare say a word — nothing — to just sit there silently until suddenly, almost angrily he'd order me to play a certain chord over and over and over and over . . . sometimes as many as twelve or fifteen times in a row and even though I was so torturously tired that I was reeling, his promptings for every note he instructed me to play kept getting more and more intense, his insults more paralyzing as he'd suddenly bang down both fists on the keyboard yelling, "Art is *nostalgia* — *idiot!* and nostalgia is *mourning!*" He'd seethe, "You have to *dream* the chord — you have to create an atmosphere of *dreaming* as though the chord were a question God were asking of the *Soul* — *can you do that?* — *Yes or No?*" he'd yell — then he'd make me play the chord again . . . and then again . . . and then again . . . because when he was composing he was insane, a madman, his face turning scarlet as tears welled up as he'd reach over from the piano bench where he was sitting and start wildly scribbling onto the enormous stacks of paper in front of him . . . and this would go on until . . . without saying a word he'd get up almost in a trance, leave . . . and then . . . in front of the window of his music room twenty minutes later . . . with one finger pointing upward he'd order me to take off my pajama top . . . then with his finger pointing downward, to drop the bottoms to the floor . . . then as I was standing naked in front of the window he'd begin watching me through his binoculars as I'd pull out my ponytail . . . as he'd motion to me to climb up on my little wooden desk chair . . . and then start turning . . . slowly . . . and then he'd motion me to bend over with my back to him . . . as he kept watching . . . watching . . . through those heavy black binoculars, his thin lips tightened into something almost sinister . . . a kind of vicious grimace, as he began doing that business to his one-eyed monster that was staring blindly into the night as though the night were a wall that could somehow protect both of us from the monstrosity of his needs, the ugliness of his passion . . . if I tried to understand what was going on with me and Maestro von Ochsenstein . . . make some kind of story of it, my mind went blank — if I tried to come to any conclusions or to put a beginning and an end together, my head would become foggy and nothing formed . . . it was all the huge amorphous now, some big blown-up instant without a past or future that felt like it would go on forever that I was drifting through without rules or limits or any meaning to anyone except to him . . . only it didn't go on forever . . . little by little . . . after all the pieces were completed he stopped coming to the window as often — after all the compositions were finally finished . . . *The Charlotte Concertos* . . . *Heartbreak* and *Night,* he began playing downstairs in the living room more and more . . . as I kept waiting in front of the window . . . waiting . . . waiting . . . until the act of waiting became another order . . . another harsh command . . . to just keep . . . waiting . . . waiting . . . until sometimes I'd fall asleep as the sun was rolling in from the bottom of the window . . . racing home from school, racing from the train station . . . across the streets, up the hill . . . across the lawn because I didn't bring his lunch to the Academy anymore because he started having lunch at home — meeting people at his house, conducting meetings . . . business . . . interviews at home . . . at home now most of the time since the tragedy.

8

"One conducts with the *Eyes!* . . . it's all in the *Eyes — the Eyes,"* I listened to him telling the packed living room filled with reporters that afternoon because of the colossal deal he had just inked with RCA records that not only made him a multimillionaire overnight, but put his face on the cover of not only *Time*, but of *Life* magazine as well . . . "which in my opinion is proof positive of the deep telepathy that exists between the orchestra and its conductor," he was telling the room packed full of people as I was standing all the way in the back . . . listening, watching . . . looking around at the crowd of photographers, reporters, cameramen — members of the orchestra — his entire staff, some of the help — the cook Mrs. Stillwaters, Crump . . . everyone fielding questions . . . talking, as I was noticing again as I was standing there, as though I had never realized . . . how tall he was . . . how pale chalky white his skin was . . . transparent almost . . . watching . . . his long bald head . . . the easy way he wore clothes . . . the way he used his hands while he was speaking . . . "and what's more," he laughed — no trace of grief — no hint . . . no sadness at all as though Charlotte Hec's suicide had been put in a drawer, the drawer had been slammed shut and that was that . . . the scent of tragedy was nowhere in the house . . . or in his life . . . he didn't suffer the same as other people . . . the same as the help were suffering . . . as I was suffering . . . as all the members of the orchestra were suffering . . . because people like Maestro Otto von Ochsenstein don't feel guilty or ever suffer — it simply isn't in their nature . . . they have some strange lacking — something vacant in them that doesn't register loss like the rest of us . . . "believe me," he was laughing, "what goes on between the orchestra and the conductor's *Eyes* is proof positive that telepathy *Does Exist! — take my word!*" his hands moving gracefully as he was speaking — those enormous hands that during a concert seemed like flowing rivers . . . "and what's more again," he went on laughing, "since we're here today to discuss the series of concerts I shall be recording early next year, all my new compositions that I've dedicated to my magnificent wife whom, as you all know, I've recently lost" he said as he looked up for a moment at the gigantic portrait of her above the fireplace . . . "I would like to begin by saying that I'm a nocturnal beast, something between a bat and Count Dracula," he joked, "creatures," he said, "who only become completely vibrant after dark," he laughed as everyone in the room began laughing with him like a quiet mindless echo that was softly following him as he walked slowly over to one of the two pianos in front of the big bay window that he had been using now almost all the time . . . "in the first place," he said as he was beaming warmly, joy seeming to completely have the upper hand that afternoon because he was in front of a large adoring crowd of worshippers which was his favorite place on earth — this is what he lived for — craved . . . "I never get up before noon," he smiled, "and I'm not emotional at noon — who is? " he laughed whole heartedly as he began pouring on his famous charm — that extremely suspicious quality . . . snakey, watery . . . unreliable — that was flowing out of him now as though he turned it on from a spigot as Charlotte Hec . . . her raving beauty . . . in a red satin nightgown, her black flying hair with no slippers on those sad heartbreaking feet . . . was still hanging by her neck as the Maestro took a sip of water, smiled and went on to say that since he composes only in the dead of night, he laughed, "which means I'm more a bat than Count Dracula," he was joking with all the reporters as they were all laughing as they were all scribbling wildly . . . "which brings us to the question," he said more seriously . . . "what is composing — what is creating — where does a beautiful piece of music come from . . . a beautiful painting . . . the novel . . . ah, such terrible questions," he laughed "questions that really can never be answered because they belong to the realm of *Magic . . . and Magic is Magic!*" he smiled, "but just for size," he said, "let's try on what the great composer and conductor Musil Mosolovitch says about composing. . . *'a great piece of music,'* he said, *'is the sum total of all the composer's experiences — his love affairs, the books he's read, his religion . . . and most of all — the country of his birth,'* — and the same can be said for a novel, a great painting — and in my case," the Maestro went on, "that aggregate of passions to create music strikes only after dark," he laughed as he leaned against one of the huge great pianos and crossed his legs as Charlotte Hec

. . . her wide-open eyes, clutching a picture in her hand of Oscar von Ochsenstein . . . was still hanging in the kitchen by the Maestro's long white satin opera scarf . . . as the Maestro was sauntering among all the reporters, shaking hands and smiling in an easy gray sweater, gray trousers, brown handmade loafers, a gray tweed jacket . . . one hand in his trouser pocket with a red satin scarf around his neck . . . lean, bald, tall, shiny and very white — this intrepid showman, this alabaster god straight out of *Life* magazine or — *Time* — shrewd, calculating . . . always on stage . . . always performing . . . his love of being looked at . . . seen . . . showing off even while he was waiting in line to buy a movie ticket . . . even in the eyeglass store, it didn't matter . . . "ah, the great Musil Mosolovitch," he went on with a soft look melting his long white marble face as he began sauntering slowly back to that magnificent orange marble fireplace that had been a gift from the Italian government in gratitude for the year he had been guest conductor in Milan . . . "Mosolovitch is a superb man! completely natural at the piano as though he and the piano are one," he continued . . . "but first and foremost, the great Mosolovitch is an *Exile! — always the Exile!* — even as he's conducting his own music from his own piano accompanied by his own magnificent orchestra — he is still the *exile* — always the exile — forever displaced — forever without a home," he said, as he flourished those great gigantic hands like they were ornaments, those enormous hands that I adored too much . . . everything about him I adored too much — there is such a thing, a dreadful terrible thing as too much mixed with an agonizing tenderness — an awful terrible tenderness because of how much he had given me — *everything* . . . passion . . . a hunger . . . lust . . . and the ecstasy of our secret life . . . that left my soul hanging over his fingers like a tattered rag . . . and knowing as I was watching him that afternoon . . . knowing . . . as I was standing in the back of his living room that day . . . knowing even then that this was my crescendo . . . that this was the one note I'd hit in my life that others could never even hear . . . and knowing too . . . that now there was nothing else for me . . . not anymore . . . not school — not friends — not a mother . . . or a father . . . or even the cello anymore — nothing . . . except Otto von Ochsenstein — this man, gigantic and terrible . . . like the towering painting above the fireplace of Charlotte Hec that was thirty times bigger than life.

"And what's more," he said, "I compose only at one piano which is in my music room," he said, "because I believe that that piano *is enchanted!*" he went on as he began strolling around the room again while he was scratching his smooth white chin that like all of him was long and thin and colorless, something so white about him — his whole body like a piece of chalk as I watched him as I stood there, wanting to consume all of him in one gigantic gulp — whatever was left of cannibalism turning into a frenzied personal desire that afternoon to inhale him, ingest him into me as I was standing in

the very back of his crowded living room that afternoon
. . . so painfully, so wildly, so horrendously in love with
him . . . especially when he was performing . . . showing
off . . . being spectacular like he was that day . . . that's
when mad adoration completely overwhelmed me . . .
I was becoming insane with admiration — sick from it
. . . (admiration can do terrible things, turn you into an
imbecile), as I suddenly wanted the whole world to know
that this astonishing man was mine . . . that he belonged
to me . . . that I was his secret wife . . . that we had a
bond . . . made secret vows that we lived by . . . night
and day . . . day and night . . . as I stood there ready to
declare . . . in front of everyone . . . to all the reporters,
all the cameramen — his staff — all the members of
the orchestra . . . his maids . . . his cook . . . wanting the
whole world to know — wanting everyone to know . . .
that this great man belonged to me — that it was I who
was his love . . . I, who not only worked on every piece
with him . . . but was going to record every piece with
him . . . perform every piece with him as we'd tour the
world . . . all the great music halls of Europe — *Me —
Hannah Elizabeth Gold* . . . as I came forward through the
crowded living room that afternoon smiling . . and then
. . . standing directly in front of him . . . still smiling . . .
waiting for my nod . . . waiting for him to point me out
to all the reporters . . . waiting . . . for him to introduce
me . . . waiting for my smile . . . waiting . . . only nothing
happened . . . not a word . . . not a nod . . . nothing . . .
as he was laughing at something someone was saying

. . . blind to the fact that I was standing directly in front of him smiling . . . waiting . . . "ah, but sadly," he said as he looked completely past me, " . . . in order to create something truly remarkable we need the magic of all those precious deities," he said . . . not seeing me . . . not seeing that I was standing there still smiling . . . as if I didn't exist . . . like Charlotte Hec didn't exist . . . like his past . . . that he could shed over and over . . . like a snake can shed its skin . . . didn't exist as he was opening his gigantic hands as though he were about to offer up some priceless treasure to all his gods to whom long ago he had turned himself over . . . "all those mighty deities," he said, "whom we must humbly beseech to allow us entry into their dark domain," he went on softly . . . "into their most secret vaults because all the magic in the world belongs to them, and *magic* it truly is," he went on quietly . . . his thick, ice blue reptilian eyes . . . like the dead blue eyes of a crocodile . . . staring blankly out into that vast sea of reporters, lost by what he was bestowing on that whole worshipful crowd . . . on all the cameramen . . . on his son Daniel who was his favorite — maybe the only one of all his children he loved . . . on Daniel's fiancée Gay Jones — on his son Oliver — on his secretary, Gazelle Dimitri-Corson . . . on the various members of the orchestra who were there that day — his staff . . . the maids . . . the cook . . . everyone hanging on every word — every gem this huge pale giant god of music was bestowing as though every word were a golden life raft floating in a sea of emerald bliss . . . as he ambled back to the two black concert grand pianos, back to back . . . and leaning against the farthest one, he said quietly . . . "and if they, all those mysterious gods and goddesses who dwell in the sanctity of bestowing great creative powers . . . if they will grant us even one small work of supreme importance . . . if indeed they sparkle us with their mystery blessings so that we may transport our livingness onto paper — into sound . . . color . . . words . . . then for one precious moment, my friends, we can lift something heavy from the human soul — the aloneness we suffer all the time, the isolation we all carry in our bosoms, our terrible sense of alienation. But we can achieve this *only* because of the work they've allowed us to give the world — So if they will, and if we can . . . for a little while," he said as he was holding out his enormous open hands to all of them . . . "we are no longer alone . . . and that, my friends," he said very quietly, "is the *magic* of art."

"Real freedom is found only in the madness of love."

OTTO VON OCHSENSTEIN

part six

thirty-three

Nine months after Charlotte Hec committed suicide, under her enormous portrait above the fireplace ... the Maestro married Gay Jones.

Juliet didn't come to the wedding and neither did any of her three half-brothers because Gay Jones was the former fiancée of Daniel von Ochsenstein, the Maestro's favorite son ... as for Gay Jones, she was anything but pretty ... hideously thin with thick black curly hair, almost frizzy, a heavily pockmarked face — overly eager, overly animated with stick-thin legs, skeletal almost in her short white lace wedding dress and red satin stiletto heels ... her small, sullen little dark-haired daughter Mona, who was ten at the time, standing next to her — she had been a salesgirl in the luggage department at John Wanamaker's when she met Daniel, and in the two and a half years they were together she was a constant presence at all the von Ochsenstein events ... and, unless looks are completely deceiving ... the Maestro was ecstatic.

No one familiar was at the wedding — not a soul — it was a whole strange new group of unfamiliar faces like new porch furniture on an old familiar porch ... as I ran from the train station that day to the Maestro's house ... then stood in the back of the living room ... watching ... my eyes riveted ... first staring at Gay Jones ... then at her little daughter Mona — then at the few members of the Maestro's staff . . . his secretary, Gazelle Dimitri-Corson . . . then at both of the Maestro's lawyers, but no one else I knew was there — not one member of the orchestra . . . not one of the Maestro's old cronies . . . not his mother, the ancient countess, not his famous brother, Sir Oscar von Ochsenstein . . . or Stella Bernstein . . . or either of his two turkey vulture sisters in all their capes and wigs . . . as I stared at Gay Jones again . . . and then at her little daughter Mona . . . as a wild jealousy began gnawing into me like teeth because of the way the Maestro was looking at her . . . *never apologize for this beauty* . . . he would tell her . . . it wouldn't be long before he'd hold her by the shoulders, his great reptilian eyes glaring into her as he'd whisper . . . *never cower . . . never cringe, never be ashamed . . . because whether you know it or not,* he'd whisper to her . . . *it's what everything in the universe hungers for* . . . as I gazed up at the enormous portrait of Charlotte Hec above the fireplace that I suddenly wanted to crawl into . . . merge with, become part of this exquisite creature — fuse with her . . . even with just her picture . . . and how after she died everything died . . . no more music out on the grass at night — no wandering bands of Russian violinists in Cossack costumes — no flowers spilling out of enormous vases everywhere . . . or movie stars and artists or writers and ballet dancers or the one or two great musicians who were always floating around their house — gone, all of it . . . as though she took it all with her . . . Juliet left for Radcliff when she was sixteen, too brilliant even for Garrison Hopkin; they didn't know what to do with her, and nor did she last at Radcliff either . . . when she was seventeen she became the youngest in an order of Franciscan nuns bound for Ireland to become monks in a remote monastery where no one spoke . . . "contemplatives," as they were called . . . I would visit her many times in the years that followed . . . stunned each time by how little they ate . . . by the way they all were dressed, both the men and the women . . . all of them in tan sackcloth with brown leather sandals — stunned, at the extremes of so much deprivation . . . and more stunned by how hideously soundless it was inside those crumbling monastery walls . . . how they all lived in absolute silence, not speaking a word until they were outside the gates, and even then they had to walk miles into the green rolling countryside before they could utter a single sound . . . and how out there Juliet seemed to come alive . . . the old Juliet again as she hugged me and began to laugh exactly the way she used to . . . and how out there in those great green rolling meadows nothing seemed changed — nothing seemed lost . . . the old times and the old ways seemed to have been recaptured . . . everything seemed to have been regained . . . except the poetry that Juliet wrote and read and recited all the time . . . the poetry that Juliet was . . . gone! — nothing was regained — nothing recaptured . . . it was an illusion . . . a terrible wrenching hope as Juliet, in her tan sackcloth with her brown leather sandals, mute and stoic waved good-bye as I drove away . . . the only joy for her now was the joy of sacrifice . . . the joy of denial . . . but this was later . . . years later . . . long after that day when Ida Jenks called me at school to tell me she learned from the Maestro's cook, Mrs. Stillwaters, that Maestro von Ochsenstein was going to be married that afternoon . . . as I grabbed my books . . . ran out of school, ran from the train station, across the street, up the hill, across the lawn . . . into the house and then stood in the back of their living room with Ida Jenks, sick with an impotent hopeless rage . . . dazed and lightheaded . . . watching . . . the backs of the Maestro and Gay Jones standing together next to each other in front of the orange marble fireplace . . . the Maestro smiling as he was kissing Gay Jones's hand . . . as I watched . . . his thick, heavy-lidded ice blue reptilian eyes like the dead eyes of a crocodile . . . gazing at Gay Jones . . . his usually hollow sunken cheeks now full as he was flashing a huge reptilian grin like the frozen grin of an alligator unable to hide its terrible hungry teeth . . . as he kissed Gay Jones's hand . . . again . . . and then again.

"Crocodilians," Mrs. Brewster told our science class, her words blazing as I was standing there . . . "are divided into three families: crocodiles, gavials and alligators — an ancient group of reptiles known for grabbing whatever they desire as they lie in wait, lurking, these great solitary monsters — nocturnal, highly temperamental and intelligent who can bring down a white-tailed deer as fast and as easily as they can break the neck of a hippo or swallow an anaconda whole without taking a single bite — these kings of stealth who will never lift a finger to help a neighbor," she smiled as she looked around the room . . . "always on the alert for new splashing sounds to trigger their insatiable appetites — these monsters . . . the ultimate predator!"

Or did he look more like "Nick," the Gila monster in the big glass tank in the back of the science room that we fed three rodents to every day . . . that was the question . . . as I stood in the back of the Maestro's living room that afternoon wondering about this the same as I wondered about my frozen hands the day we found Aunt Charlotte . . . *"one of only two species of venomous lizards,"* Mrs. Brewster smiled as she stood in front of the blackboard with a pointer in her hand . . . a huge lowered picture of a giant Gila monster glaring at us. . ."*usually found under rocks or in the burrows of other animals — feeds on small mammals,"* she said, *"its excess fat stored in its enormous bulging tail,"* she told our class as I was staring at Maestro von Ochsenstein's bald shiny head as he kept smiling at Gay Jones with that same look on his face as when he was conducting anything by his idol . . . the great Russian composer Musil Mosolovitch — how everything by Mosolovitch filled the Maestro with a kind of ecstasy that made him immediately soften . . . which was how he looked when he looked at her . . . *"both species of these venomous lizards have a strong, tenacious bite,"* Mrs. Brewster smiled, *"with teeth that have two thick grooves that conduct the venom, which is a rare nerve toxin that comes from the glands in the lower jaw . . . the toxin is not injected like that of the snake,"* she was smiling as she was gazing sightlessly at me as she was telling us this, *"but instead,"* she said, *"it flows into the wounds as the lizard slowly chews its victim to death,"* . . . as they all began parading in front of me . . . Alligators! Iguanas! Crocodiles! Gila monsters . . . all flashing their hideous pointy teeth . . . all flapping their ugly bulging tails — despicable, solitary monsters . . . nocturnal . . . selfish . . . self-centered and highly temperamental — these ultimate predators . . . as I stood in the back of the Maestro's living room that day with Ida Jenks, clutching my pile of schoolbooks into me as the ceremony began.

Musil Mosolovitch
cello concerto in D Major
with
Musil Mosolovitch
conducting the
Moscow Philharmonic

Hannah Elizabeth Gold, cello

This is what I'm remembering... all these things always going through my mind... always thinking about them ... haunted by them... as I walk out on stage carrying my grandmother's cello, and always to a wondrous reception — always to a thunderously welcoming applause... and every time I walk out — every time I sit down... for a moment... I see the big staring eyes, like the glowing incandescent eyes of an iguana... or a crocodile... watching me... and it's always to those eyes... to that chalk-white face and long bald head that might be out there this time... that I give myself over to as if to some golden deity... some pale white god who might be standing all the way in the back of the house tonight, without whom there could be no music... no enchantment... as I place my grandmother's cello between my knees... take my A from whomever the concert master is that evening — wherever I happened to be playing — in whatever country — city... as I look out into that gray sea of faces again... sure I'll see him someday... sure someday he'll turn up — how could he not?

I dreamed about this all the time; for years I dream the same dream — that one day he'll come back and then everything will be exactly like it was... the two of us playing like we did that night in Paris in his little golden palace before the huge white house next door was sold... before my father and my mother were gone... even before my debut at the Cathedral of Saint Sebastian when he came backstage after our performance . . . and kissed the tips of all my fingers . . . every finger.

In my dream it all comes alive as he's holding my hand high up in the air as everyone keeps clapping clapping clapping clapping; then the dream changes and he's in a yellow satin dressing gown with a bright green satin scarf around his neck peering at me from the top of the Eiffel Tower through enormous black binoculars . . . laughing . . . laughing . . . or I dream he's peering at me from the empty stage at the Academy of Music with no one in the audience except me . . . standing on one of the empty seats in my pajamas — or else he's peering into our dining room as he's standing naked on our side of the hedges, playing with that monster with one hand while in the other he's holding the binoculars, only in the dream the binoculars are two enormous black torpedoes — how old was I then, I wonder as I'm watching the conductor as I'm waiting for my cue . . . maybe twelve when I started bringing his lunch to the Academy every day . . . remembering walking up the steps, remembering the excitement — remembering my heart pounding as I was walking down that long gray hall wondering the whole time if my shoes were clean as I was taking out my ponytail as I walked into that dim brown room carrying his crab cake and his ice cold Coke, and knowing even then . . . even when I was still so young . . . even when I was still only just a child . . . that those were my best years . . . as I'd climb up on his desk in that dreary little chamber at the Academy exactly the way he instructed me with one finger twirling as he'd gaze at me through those heavy black binoculars while he was sitting right beside me . . . right next to me — even in there . . . staring at me through his black binoculars with me on top of his desk right next to him stripped down to just my garter belt and those thick woolen stockings the color of pale flesh that children used to wear as I'd start turning slowly . . . as I was holding up my hair while he sat naked in the chair beside me . . . caressing his monster with one hand as he kept gazing at me through those black binoculars . . . until he'd beckon me down from the top of his desk, and then on my knees in front of him . . . his legs wide apart, his eyes closed, his head all the way back — those memories of all the memories, those memories — the most depraved and corrupt, the lowest — the most debased . . . became with time the most cherished, the most treasured and prized . . . those memories of all the memories . . . still gleaming in the shadows like exquisite jewels — the indelibleness of them still shining through the mist of time — memories of the passion, the need — the hunger . . . the frenzy, the lust and the ecstasy . . . he gave me everything because he gave me *that!* as he'd pull me into the couch in his chamber at the Academy . . . onto the pale satin couch in his living room when no one was close by, in the house but not close by . . . into the sofa upstairs in his music room — when Crump was driving on the backseat of that long black Chrysler New Yorker —

pounding! — banging! — banging! — pounding! — remembering once how the rubber broke and he just kept going, racing — tearing — it didn't matter, nothing mattered because it was too good to stop he said as I was crying because it felt like he was pounding open one door in me after the next after the next — doors that could never again be shut as he was laughing, laughing . . . throwing his head all the way back and laughing as we walked out on stage together . . . the fast bold way we walked out holding hands and laughing . . . he holding my hand so tight it hurt because I was trembling from the terrifying thrill of having just performed with Otto von Ochsenstein conducting the great Philadelphia Philharmonic — maybe the greatest orchestra in the world as we turned to the audience and bowed . . . then bowed again . . . and then again . . . how old was I . . . thirteen — maybe fourteen by then; if I never married it was because I was married to the music . . . married to that other gift he gave me, and she gave me too — Stella Bernstein . . . one of the finest cellists in the world . . . and oddly — only after she died did I begin to hear what I was playing . . . only then . . . after she was gone . . . for the first time I began to hear the grandeur, the majesty of every piece as though suddenly all of it . . . everything I ever played . . . everything I ever studied, everything I ever heard in my whole life came soaring out of her grave as though to protect and envelope me in an iron cocoon — a magnificent majestic cocoon made of music . . . as the horror of Stella

Bernstein in a blood-soaked nightgown . . . the horror of her car smashed into a tree . . . a horror that reached out to grab hold of me and stay . . . like the clothes I wear . . . like my coat . . . like the scarf around my head . . . always there . . . always "upon me" all the time to remind me that as the Maestro said . . . *there isn't happy or unhappy — either there's strength or there's weakness — so choose Strength! — Strength!* he'd blast . . . because people don't recover from anything, they just go on in some other way like Juliet in her tan sackcloth and brown leather sandals waving good-bye with no expression . . . her blank face like a piece of empty paper flashing in front of me as I look up at the conductor . . . whichever great conductor . . . whomever the conductor is that night — then glance out into the audience for a moment, thinking maybe I'll see him leaning against a pillar all the way in the back — maybe I'll see him standing up in the back of a box upstairs . . . sure he'd turn up — maybe tonight . . . maybe tomorrow night — next week, next month standing near the exit all the way in the back . . . as I'm remembering after my father died, how my mother began telling everyone that I was in Alcatraz because I had tried to kill her, these thoughts . . . fragments . . . coming in bits . . . then drifting as I keep my eye on the conductor — her sad diagnosis was a wild paranoia unhinged by booze as a shadow fell over her that never went away . . . from that day on it was as though she operated under a cloud — it was she I'm thinking as I look up at the conductor . . . she who

was my lifelong fascination with reptiles — my mother
... the female cobra who ran from her hatchlings
because she was terrified of eating them ... or was it
Maestro von Ochsenstein the day he married Gay Jones
... when I wanted to crawl into that enormous portrait
above the fireplace of Charlotte Hec ... into her arms
... into her mouth ... be swallowed into her and
disappear ... or did my fascination with reptiles begin
as I kept staring at the Maestro's eyes that afternoon
that were like the glowing ice-blue iridescent eyes of a
crocodile ... unblinking, seeing only his prey ... those
big glassy eyes blazing with that familiar same cold-blue
flame as he stared at Gay Jones, instead of me — was
that when I chose strength — in all my rage and jealousy
— in all my torment ... because I didn't crawl into the
portrait of Charlotte Hec ... I never crawled into the
portrait of Charlotte Hec ... not even as I watched him
turn his all-entitled gaze toward her little daughter
Mona ... I just stood there ... as rage and jealousy,
furious hideous jealousy, a heartbreaking terrible
jealousy swept through me ... as I clutched my
schoolbooks into me so hard that day that I broke all
my fingernails ... as the conductor, whomever the
conductor is that night ... Adolph Becker, Robert Lord
... Maurice Dry of the Chicago Philharmonic cues my
entrance into the Dvořák, as Charlotte Hec still hangs
by the Maestro's long white satin opera scarf as his
fame keeps only growing ... his immense good luck
and colossal fortune ... his new music even more

magnificent . . . with Gay Jones's sullen little daughter Mona staying on . . . "ah, to be seventy-five again," I later learned is the way the Maestro always introduces little Mona, this is the joke, always the same . . . which is what I'm thinking as I keep watching the conductor . . . Eugene Sopha this week, Charles Welty the following . . . Arthur Stone of the London Orchestra the week after that . . . for my nod . . . my cue . . . as all these thoughts . . . all these little islands that keep popping up . . . as I walk out on stage holding hands with the magnificent Andre Stern . . . as we bow . . . then bow again . . . with Vladimir Grass . . . with Milos Chodov as we bow . . . then bow again . . . and then again to standing ovations every night — every night to cheers and bravos as they keep applauding, thunderously applauding, wildly applauding as the house lights come on . . . what the Maestro gave me might not have been everything, but it was, as he would say, *Enough* . . . because he loved me . . . which made those years the best years of my life . . . I'm smiling as I look out over that great gray sea of faces all up on their feet . . . all applauding, with still more cheers and bravos as they keep applauding . . . thunderously applauding . . . wildly applauding . . . as I'm holding hands with Kurt Mazel . . . as we bow . . . then bow again . . . and then again.

Then toward the end of December, it was at Carnegie Hall — we had just performed Mosolovitch's Cello Concerto in D Major . . . the great Russian composer, by then well into his eighties conducting the Moscow Philharmonic, himself only a few years older than von Ochsenstein — Musil Mosolovitch — maybe one of the greatest composers and conductors ever, whom von Ochsenstein worshipped his whole life, a huge photograph of him from a time when they both were young, both strong and strident had always hung over the Maestro's desk. It was on that evening that I saw . . . standing all the way in the back of the house — leaning against a pillar . . . the towering form — the long bald head . . . and big staring eyes, like the glowing incandescent eyes of an iguana or a crocodile . . . in a black coat, and long white satin opera scarf . . . as we walked out together — I and the great Mosolovitch . . . my heart pounding with the thrill — the excitement . . . that for that one instant . . . for that one shining moment . . . it was he . . . as I and the great Mosolovitch bowed . . . then bowed again . . . and then again.